POWER LOSS

POWER LOSS

TODD CINANI
AMBER BENBOW
SHAUN CURTIS
ASHLEY LAINO
MAX MCCAMISH
JUSTIN ALCALA
SILENCIO MARQUEZ
PATRICK TILLETT
EDITED BY JOHN WAIT

BLKDOG

www.blkdogpublishing.com

THE DAY OF THE BLACKOUT IS REMEMBERED AS DAY ZERO.

THE LAST PHONE CALL

BY TODD CINANI

DAY 0

The sunlight pours in through the window, hitting my eyes like an anvil. *Jesus, my head hurts.* I'm desiccated like a smoked trout. I vaguely remember dancing to Funky Town. Tied one on last night. Checking the bed to make sure I'm alone, I struggle to sit upright. *The pain.* Okay, I'm mostly upright now. Looking around, I notice the alarm clock is off. Grabbing the remote, I click it to turn on the TV. Nothing. Okay, TV out too. Power must be out. Don't know if it's our apartment building or the whole block.

Staggering into the kitchen, I confirm the fridge is also off. So yeah, no power. That means no hot water, and I really need a shower. Pondering this for a moment, I decide maybe a cold shower will help with the hang over. …

Okay, that was mostly awful and there is no heat, so I'm curled under a blanket for warmth. I downed a Gatorade before the shower so I feel a bit better. Phone won't turn on. Battery must be dead. That sucks ass. I can't charge it. Now I have no entertainment. I can't even read because all my books are digital. Maybe I should call the power company. Yeah, that's what I'll do. See how long the power will be off.

Landline is dead too. What the hell? They are supposed to work when the power is off. Looking at the router, I can see the land line plugged into it. Oh yeah, all the land lines go through cable or your internet provider now. If the power is out, they don't work either. So I have been paying for a fucking landline in case this happens, and it's worthless. *I'm an idiot.* I should have thought about that. Well, I'm canceling the land line the minute everything comes back on.

It's quiet. Too quiet, I think remembering the line from some movie or several. Looking out the window I see no cars, just people in groups talking and holding their cell phones high in the air. Good luck. If the power outage is extensive, most cell towers are out too. At least you can access games or something saved on the phone. I should go outside. *I don't feel like it.* I have some Chinese in the fridge I should eat before it goes bad.

I'm sitting on the couch with the Chinese on the coffee table. I stir the Sweet & Sour Pork, wishing the TV worked. I hate this. *The silence.* It stresses me out. Wind stresses me out too, but I'd take that over the silence. It's starting to get dark. Maybe the crickets will start to chirp. I pick up the takeout cartons and toss them in the trash. Screw this, I'm just going to bed. Sleep through the boredom and hope everything is right with the world tomorrow.

DAY 4

Four days later and still no power. I've slept a lot and eaten what I could from the fridge that didn't need to be cooked. There's still a steak in there I'm considering. I think I can make a grill out of a big pot and an oven rack and grill it on the roof.

I did go down to the street yesterday and talked to some people in the neighborhood. Nobody really knows what is going on, and odder still there has been no news from the power company or the city. People are starting to get edgy. Apparently, none of the cars work either. It is frustrating not knowing.

Bang, bang, bang goes the door. What's this now? I open the door and there's Alvie standing there, a stressed look on his face.

"Alvie! What's up?"

"Hey cousin, we gotta go."

"What? What are you talking about?"

"I've been driving around trying to figure out what's going on…" Alvie walks into the apartment and I shut the door.

"Wait. You've been driving? I thought the cars were…"

"It's my old truck. Got it started rolling it downhill. It's still running downstairs, but I locked the doors. Get your stuff. Clothes and essentials only."

"Why? What's going on?"

"People are starting to lose it. Robbing, rioting and killing. I've seen some fucked up shit."

"Jesus." *This is crazy.* It's only been a few days and the city is starting to descend into chaos?

"So, let's get the fuck outta dodge."

I grab lots of underwear and socks, a sweater, jeans and shirts and throw them in a bag. Alvie is in the kitchen raiding the canned food.

We exit the apartment and head downstairs. Once on the street, I see Alvie's rusted old truck. It has started to draw a crowd. We have to shove our way through and toss the bags in the back. People are asking why the truck is running. Alvie shouts out, "It's old!"

We take to the streets dodging the stationary cars that must have died en route to wherever they were going. The streets are mostly empty, but occasionally a group runs across. We see shattered store front windows. Alvie's right. The looting's started. *Shit, was that a gunshot?* Okay, that was definitely a series of gunshots, closer than I would like.

Alvie turns this way and that, not slowing at the intersections. I have no idea where we're going. But Alvie seems determined, like he knows what he was doing. So I let him drive, while I watch out the window a city I no longer recognize.

We see a military Hum-Vee coming toward us down the street. Suddenly, the street between us rises in a bulge and cracks apart, spouting fire like a volcano. The Hum-Vee swerves off and crashes straight into a storefront. I yell for Alvie to stop but he is already hitting the breaks to avoid the eruption. I hop out of the truck as it comes to a stop on instinct alone. *There's no thought.*

"What the fuck…?" Alvie yells after me.

I run over to the Hum-Vee. A soldier staggers out of the rear driver's side door. She is dazed. I yell to her, asking if she's okay. She looks back at me confused. I ask again. Slowly the confusion leaves her eyes and they clear, filled with purpose. She dives into the back seat towards a man in a suit.

He's leaned up against the back of the front seat with his neck and head at an unnatural angle. His eyes are open but unseeing. I move towards the front door and peer in. The driver's head has gone through the windshield. His helmet is pushed back and the skin on his face is peeled off like in some grotesque horror film, oozing eyes and all muscle and bone. I immediately turn and vomit. The soldier scoots out of the back seat and pushes me aside as she opens the driver's door. She yanks the driver's head out of the glass and tosses him on the ground. I look up and see her fellow soldier in the passenger seat. He has the broken shaft of a golf club embedded in his eye socket. The handle of the club is still in the windshield which appears to be the only thing keeping him upright. *Oh, they've crashed into a sporting goods store…*

I take some steps back. I notice Alvie grabbing two gas cans from the rear of the Hum-Vee and running them over to the truck. The soldier is harvesting the bodies for weapons and ammo. I just stand motionless, dazed. *What is going on?* How did I go from getting up in the morning, sleepy and bored, to a war zone? In just a few hours? A series of booms interrupts my thoughts, and I see the building next to the crater spout fire and glass from its windows, each floor in rapid succession.

"Let's get the fuck outta here!" I hear the yell coming from my throat.

The soldier has already tossed the guns and ammo into the back of the truck and is hopping into the bed. I run and dive into the cab. Alvie has already put the truck in gear and is speeding backwards away from the conflagration. Once far enough away Alvie flawlessly spins the tuck in a 180 and we are speeding forward. We make a right and speed on.

"What the hell was that?" I ask Alvie.

"Looked like a gas main blew up. I don't know. Maybe without power there's nothing to pump it and it builds up or something." *As good an explanation as any.* I look in the passenger rear view window and watch more explosions erupt randomly about the city scape. It looks like the end of the world.

***

We're in the industrial district on the outskirts of the city and decide to stop for the night and figure out a plan. Up until now the only plan had been to get out of the chaos. Alvie pulls up to what looks like a garage or warehouse. We get out of the truck. The building has a rollup door, and Alvie notices the deadbolt locking it. He goes back to the truck to pull out bolt cutters from amongst various other tools behind the seat. The soldier stands up in the bed of the truck, gun at the ready, instinctively doing guard duty. No one is about. With no power, I guess there is not much point in people working here.

After some effort Alvie cuts the bolt and I help him push the door up. Inside it's mostly empty except for a few crates and a cargo container. Without speaking we get back into the truck and drive into the warehouse.

Once we're inside the soldier hops out of the back and pulls the door down. It is dark except for the truck's headlights throwing two beams through the floating dust. "We'll need to make a fire unless we want to sit in the dark all night," Alvie says. Without speaking the soldier walks over to a wooden crate and starts prying it open with her knife. I decide to check out the cargo container. As I walk over to it, little clouds of dust erupt from each footfall. The place must have been vacant for a few years.

The cargo container is latched but not locked. I pull on the latch and open one of the doors. It is loaded with cardboard boxes. I pull out a box and use my apartment key to tear through the tape. The box is full of plush round dolls, those Japanese Peki Dude dolls that were so popular about a decade ago. I remember they went with some game that was all the rage at the time. They're worthless now. I dump them out and toss the box towards the truck. I do the same with several others boxes. Cardboard burns. Our soldier is doing the same with the wooden crates, which seem to be packed with antiques, vases, small statues and other expensive and delicate-looking items. All surrounded with that shredded paper straw. She's gathering up a bunch of it and walking over to where I tossed the boxes.

Soon we have a decent fire going and sit by it. I gaze at the antiques illuminated by the flickering flames. *Where had they been?* What type of owner did they have, and what drama occurred in the house or palace they once lived in? This glowing dancing light caressing them must have been the light they were used to at night, back in a time before electricity. *Does it soothe them?*

"We have beans and beans with some crackers if anyone is interested." Alvie comes to the fire carrying two cans and a box of crackers after rummaging through the truck. "Uhhh, I just realized I don't have a can opener." Alvie looks down at the cans with some despair. "In the craziness, I didn't even think about it."

"Here, give me." The soldier reaches towards the cans. Alvie hands her one. She whips out her knife, stabs the top of the can and starts cutting through the tin. In a bit we are using the knife to spread refried beans on crackers for dinner. It's surprisingly good.

"I think it's time for introductions," I say. "This is my cousin Alvie." I wave my hand in his direction. Alvie nods. "And I am Gerald. You can call me Ger but not Gerry. I fucking hate Gerry."

The soldier smiles. "I'm Corporal Rosalina Alonso Morales but you can call me Rosa."

"Nice to meet you, Rosa." I respond. When she smiles, she is less intimidating than when she wears the hawk-like determined expression, the only one I've seen until now.

"Well, Rosa," Alvie asks. "What were you guys doing out there in that Hum-Vee and how did you get it to work in the first place?"

"No real electronics other than a radio and GPS. GPS was fried but we could kickstart the Hum-Vee. Once it's running the generator does all the work." She explained. "We were escorting the Deputy Chief of the DOD to our HQ."

"The guy in the back?" I ask.

"Yes." She looks off into the distance.

"Where's the HQ?" Alvie said, suddenly hopeful.

"Don't know exactly. The guys up front knew, but with the GPS I could tell you. I was just the muscle to keep the Chief safe. Guess I failed at that."

After letting that sink in, we start talking about plans. We decide to take the highway to somewhere less populated, or somewhere with power. *There must be power somewhere.* I refuse to end up on some backwoods road, citing several inbred hillbilly horror movies. We decide on the plains or desert in the West, stopping in small towns for supplies if they look safe.

The fire starts to die out and we decide to sleep. I roll up some cardboard and use it as a pillow and try to drift off. For the first time today, I have time to think. In all the craziness and chaos, I've been operating on action only. Just doing. Now things are starting to sink in. My life, my friends, the girls I was flirting with, all up in smoke. How could this happen so fast? A deep sadness rushes over me, pulling me underwater like some tentacled arm dragging me down to the darkness. I see the driver's skinless face and a chill racks my body. My stomach feels painfully hollow. Not hunger but dread like I've never felt before. I'm with Alvie and Rosa, but I feel totally alone. A loneliness like no other I have every felt. Waves of anxiety wash over me and I lie in a fetal position, sweating and shivering, longing for dawn.

DAY 5

Finally, the night is over, and we leave the warehouse, heading to the nearest highway. Everything is eerily quiet and lifeless. The highway is oddly vacant except for a few cars that looked like they just rolled to a stop. We easily avoid them. When everything stopped it must have been in the middle of the night, or the highway would be full. An uneasiness settles in my bones, taking up camp, and I can feel my muscles tense. *It feels like end times.* Looking to the back to the bed of the truck I can see Rosa fiddling with a black rectangle. It looks like a phone, but it is twice as thick. She keeps touching the screen, waiting for a minute then touches it again. Whatever it is it seems to be working... or maybe not judging by the sudden frustrated expression on her face.

We have to refill with the gas cans from the Hum-Vee. After that we take turns siphoning gas from the cars we find sitting on the highway like tombstones. Eventually the trees and hills fade out and we emerge onto the flat brown plains. The highway narrows to two lanes in each direction. There are occasional farmhouses in the distance, and little roads that veer off towards some unknown destination. Alvie decides to pull over and get his bearings. He pulls out an old map of this area of the Midwest. The glove box is full of old maps. *A testament to the time before GPS.* He unfolds the map on the hood of the truck.

"As far as I can tell, based on where we were and what I have seen, we should be about here." Alvie points at a stretch of highway. "Doesn't look like much is around."

"That looks like it may be a town. No name so it must be small." Rosa points at a dot in the highway. "We'll need to restock. So, it may be a good place to check out, with caution."

"Yeah, we need something besides refried beans and crackers, tomato soup, canned peaches and cereal." Alvie gives me a disapproving look.

"Hey, I eat out a lot." I respond. Then I ask, "Rosa, what was that thing I saw you fiddling with back there?" I nod to the truck bed.

"What, this?" She pulls out the black rectangle. "It's a phone."

"Good luck." Alvie smiles. "They are all dead. Cell towers are down, batteries fucked."

"Not this one. It's satellite and shielded against just about everything. The exterior is some new carbon fiber that is stronger than titanium."

"How come the batteries still work?"

"It runs on extremely efficient kinetic energy. Every movement charges it. It's only for high-level officials."

"The Deputy Chief." I state this more than ask it.

"Yes, it's what I was looking for at the crash."

"Have you been able to reach anyone?" Hope shoots up for a millisecond.

"No. I don't even know who I'm calling. There's no names or phone numbers, just six-digit codes." *Back down again.*

We decide going forward to take turns driving and sitting in the bed of the truck. Rosa's driving and I'm in the bed. Alvie is sleeping in the passenger seat. Rosa had given me the phone to keep myself entertained. I'm to bang on the rear window if someone answers, so she can take the call. She's right. No phone numbers, no names, just a list of six-digit codes. Each has some numbers that are bigger or different colors than the other digits. I scroll through for a bit.

There must be hundreds. I decide to start at the top and work my way down. After an hour or so we slow down, pull off the road and stop behind the some large bushes and a tree. I get out my keys and scratch the last number I tried into the paint on the truck bed. The old truck is scuffed up and rusting in places, so I'm not concerned about the paint job.

"What's up?" I ask, as Rosa and Alvie get out of the cab.

"We've come to that town or whatever." Rosa waves her hand in the general direction of the road ahead.

"Yeah, we figured it would be better to walk in rather than roll up in a working vehicle." Alvie explained.

"Good idea."

"Here, take these just in case." Rosa gives us each a handgun, taken from the dead soldiers in the Hum-Vee. She then stores the other assault rifles and ammo behind the back seat with Alvie's tools. She's in her full gear.

"I don't even know how to use this." I look at the black hunk of deadly metal in my hand.

"Point it at someone and pull the trigger if things get out of hand. No time to train you now."

"If things get out of hand?"

"Look, I'm not expecting to have trouble but all the rules have changed." Rosa covers her shiny black hair with her helmet.

Alvie points the gun at the tree. "45. Yeah, I've fired these at the range. I was pretty good." I detect a slight eye roll from Rosa.

We start walking down the road. Occasionally, Rosa surveys the building shimmering in the distance through the scope of her rifle. We are about a mile away. Not too far but it will take a minute to get there. I have butterflies in my stomach. Alvie and I have our guns tucked into our rear waistbands, out of sight. I am just hoping the gun doesn't go off and shoot me in the ass. You always hear about some idiot putting his gun in his pants and shooting his balls off or something. I decide if I am going to shoot myself the ass is probably better than the crotch, and relax slightly.

We start to get close enough to make out the buildings. Rosa looks through the scope again. "Looks like it's not much better than a truck stop," Rosa notes. "We have a truck gas station, a diner, convenience store, what looks like a feed or hardware store and a garage. There's some guy driving a tracker down the street and there are people standing or walking around. Not many, four or five."

"So, what's the plan?" I ask nervously.

"I say we hit the diner first. I'm starving." Alvie rubs his stomach.

"Assuming they have food." Rosa lets the rifle hang at her side. "Not a bad idea though. We could see if anyone has any info on the road ahead."

"Yeah, then we hit the convenience store and stock up." Alvie adds.

"Again, assuming they have stock left."

We get to the truck stop. I feel like we were strangers walking into a town in the old west. People stop and give us looks. Rosa is getting some attention with her combat uniform and the assault rifle she casually holds at her side. We walk straight to the diner; I try to give a non-confrontational smile as we walk past the people staring at us. Up ahead on the road the tracker is leaving. We enter the diner like walking into a saloon, and everyone stops what they are doing and stares at us. There are three rough-looking types sitting at the counter, an old couple in a booth, a guy sitting alone in a far booth and a waitress behind the counter. She wears forty years of working in this place etched on her face. Her wiry hair is pulled up in a bun.

"Go ahead sit wherever you like." She breaks the silence and tension. The customers go back to leaning over their plates. We take the booth at equal distances from the old couple and the lone man. Rosa sits on one side, Alvie and I on the other. She puts the rifle on the table, next to the napkins and salt and pepper shakers.

The waitress come from around the counter to greet us. "How y'all doing?"

We each state that we are fine.

"You come here on horse and buggy?"

"On foot." Alvie responds.

"Oh, you poor dears. You must be starving. We ain't got much with the freezer and walk-in being off and all, but the gas still works so we can cook. We managed to salvage most of the ground beef because it was frozen when everything went off. I can do you some burgers with or without cheese. We also have powdered eggs, canned fruit salad and soup."

"I'll take a cheeseburger and some of that fruit salad." Alvie says. Rosa and I both say we'll have the same.

"Make mine well-done." I don't want to take any chances with what is probably suspect meat.

"Yeah...I think we all will have our burgers well." Alvie agreed.

"Okay. Three cheeseburgers, well-done, and three fruit salads." She pulls her pad out and makes some notes. "And what would you like to drink? We've got water, sun tea and warm beer."

"I'll take a beer and a water." I figured the beer would calm me down, take the edge off. "Make that two beers."

"I'll try the sun tea," Rosa says, and Alvie orders the same.

"Beer?" Alvie questions.

"Look I'm about this close..." I hold my thumb and forefinger about a centimeter apart. "... to having a full-on anxiety attack right here in this dinner. I need something to take the edge off."

"Yeah, okay."

Our food and drinks come. The burgers are definitely well-done, to the point of being carbon, but at least we won't get food poisoning. The beer's cheap domestic stuff, which warm tastes slightly like vomit. I drink both quickly and start to feel a bit relaxed. We finish our meal and wait for the check. At that point one of the guys at the counter comes over to our table. He's wearing a baseball cap, with a handgun on the front and the name of a local gun club crudely stiched into it. Unwashed brown hair sprouts here and there from under the cap. He puts both hands on the edge of our table and leans over towards Rosa.

"You know how to use that big gun, sweet cheeks?" He half-snarls through dark rotting teeth.

"You want to find out?" Rosa gives him a serious no-nonsense look. "It would take me all of ten seconds to shoot the balls off you and your buddies if you call me sweet cheeks again."

"Oooh…" He stands up, removing his hands from the table. "Not friendly, huh? Well, you all have a nice day." And with that he goes back to his friends at the counter, and they all have a chuckle. Thank god for the beer. My heart's pounding, but it would be much worse if not for the little buzz I have going.

"Don't mind him." The waitress came to the table with the check. "He just has no education and was beat as a kid by his drunk parents. You can pay at the register."

Shit, *pay*? I just realized I never picked up my wallet when we rushed out of the apartment. I lean toward the center of table. "Guys, I don't have any money."

"Me, neither." Rosa admitted.

"Don't worry, I have a couple of hundred." Alvie whispers as he reaches into his pocket. Thank god for Alvie, he's always prepared.

We pay for our meal and head out towards the convenience store. Rosa stops.

"Hey Alvie, can I have a hundred?"

"Uhhh, why?"

"I'm going to check out the hardware store."

"Sure, yeah, okay." Alvie hands her the money. Rosa heads across the street to the hardware store while we continue to the convenience store. Once inside, we see the shelves are pretty bare. Before, when we saw it from a distance, we'd imagined a fully stocked store with florescent lights. Instead the only light dimly falls through the window, the shelves are sparsely populated with anything useful. Lots of motor oil and antifreeze, plastic plates, a few cans of beets are the first items I notice. I grab the plates.

"You got any food?" I ask the tall, lanky kid behind the counter. Alvie is wandering through the aisles.

"There's them beets." I wince inwardly. "I think there's a couple packs of hot dogs in one of the coolers. There's some frozen pizza and burritos that ain't froze no more. We got some orange pop nobody likes. Look around, see what you can find."

I grab a basket by the door and load the beets into it. Last resort food at best. I go to the coolers. Milk, that's a no. I find the hot dogs, precooked, so they are fine. Orange pop. May as well grab them so we have something to drink. He's right about the frozen pizzas and burritos, they're warm. Pizza is out, but I pick up the burritos and look at the ingredients; beans, cheese and the usual chemicals you can barely pronounce. They should be okay, so I toss them in the basket. Alvie has found a couple of crushed boxes of cereal and a smushed bag of bagels. That is the extent of the haul.

At the register we ask the kid some questions about the road ahead, and whether a lot of people had come through here recently. The next town is a couple hundred miles and there are gas stations and rest stops between here and there. The stations are all closed because the pumps are all electric. As far as strangers coming through, there's us and a few stragglers, but that is it. The local farmers bought everything in the shop.

We leave and stand in the vacant parking lot. No sign of Rosa yet. I start to get nervous.

"Maybe we should go and check. Make sure she's okay," I tell Alvie.

"She's okay. If something went wrong, we would have heard gunfire."

"Excuse me." The lone patron from the dinner is walking up to us, backpack slung over his shoulder. He looks a few years younger than me. "I noticed how you handled that jerk back there. Those guys have been eyeing me like a piece of meat."

Alvie and I glance at each other.

"I was wondering if I could walk with you at least until we get a safe distance away."

"Uhhh… well. We have to see what our partner says," Alvie responds hesitantly.

Rosa comes out of the hardware store, carrying an ax in one hand and a large bag in the other. We move to meet her in the middle of the road.

"Rosa, this is… Sorry what's your name?" Alvie looks back at the man.

"Alex."

"This is Alex, he's afraid of the guys in the diner and was wondering if he could travel with us for a bit. Until it's safe."

"Raise your arms." Alex raises his arms and Rosa drops the bag, tossing the ax onto it. She walks over and pats him down, then takes his pack and searches it. "Okay. Follow us."

And with that the four of us head back to the truck. Once there I explain the truck to Alex while Alvie and Rosa store our supplies. Besides the ax, Rosa bought three tents and sleeping bags. Then we push the truck back to the road. I'm pretty sure everyone is glad we have an extra pair of hands. Once on the road we kick start it to get the motor running and hop in. It's my turn to drive, Rosa is sitting next to me, Alvie and Alex are sitting in the bed.

"It's probably a good I idea to drive as fast as you can through the truck stop." I have similar thoughts. As we get close, I hit the gas and we fly through at around seventy miles an hour. As we pass, I catch a glimpse of the three rough guys from the diner watching us go by from the side of the road. I think I see a smile on Redcap's face, and my stomach turns a bit.

We drive through the next town and it's eerily deserted. *A ghost town overnight.* There may be people hiding out in their houses, but we do not see anyone. The stores on the main street have been looted, windows shattered. We aren't going to find anything useful, so we decide not to risk it and keep driving.

DAY 6

As before we fill the truck and gas cans with the juice we suck from the dead cars on the road, which is now just two lanes, one each way. Occasionally we see farmhouses off the road and several vast fields of corn. I get to know Alex, and I become fast friends with Rosa. Alex had belonged to one of the vagrant cars we passed. He says he thought it was about three in morning when it died. He'd waited to mid-day for someone to come by but no one did so he grabbed his backpack and started walking. He'd been on his way to stay with his girlfriend for a few months. Meanwhile I keep trying the phone and marking whichever code I stop on in the paint of the truck bed.

We pull into a rest stop to have a break and eat the burritos. Rosa goes into the recycling bin and starts pulling out bottles and cans. *Odd.*

"Okay, guys, I think it's time to start a little shooting practice just in case." She sets the cans and bottles up on a bench, then walks over to the truck and pulls out the other two assault rifles. They are a little smaller than hers, which is slight longer and has a larger scope. These have small scopes. She does something to the guns then hands them over to us. I aim through the scope at the bottles, there's a little red light in the center that pinpoints my aim.

"Are these those AR15s the crazy people use to shoot up the joint?" I ask.

"No, AR15s are similar to my M16, these are HK416s. Special forces such as the Seals use them. Those guys in the front seat were Rangers." She sighs. "Shit way to go."

"Okay, so these guns will keep firing as long as you hold the trigger down. Don't do that. Ideally you only want to fire three round bursts like this." Rosa shoots a fast, short volley, and a bottle explodes. "Pull the trigger and release fast. Now you try, Ger."

I aim at a can using the red dot as my guide and pull the trigger. The gun goes off and I almost drop it in shock. The can's untouched but the bench has some holes.

"Okay, we'll have to work on you a bit. Alvie, you give it a try."

Alvie aims and then suddenly his gun goes off much the same way Rosa's did. His bottle also explodes. I start to feel like the kid who gets picked last in gym, but hey that was the first time I ever fired a gun, much less and assault HK whatchamacallit.

"I told you I used to go to the range." Alvie proudly lowers his gun.

"Yes, you did." Rosa smiles. "Alex, you want to give it a try?"

"Oh no, not me. I am strictly anti-gun." Alex puts his palms forward in a gesture that says get back.

We practice shooting the guns, both the HKs and the handguns. Rosa works directly with me, joking about my ability in between giving me encouragement. I think she thinks my lack of survival skills is cute. I'm like her puppy she trains not to pee on the floor. I don't think she's cute. I think she's amazing. There is nothing hotter than a woman who can kick ass.

Rosa had told me a bit about herself. As we were driving down the straight road, both of us in the cab, we talked. The conversation had started with me concerned that somehow we had gotten off the highway and were now on a regular road. Rosa got out the map and said it was a possibility because things didn't look right.

Eventually she had started to ask me questions. I told her about my life in the city, my friends, how I was in between jobs but had enough money for a few months before I had to start worrying. Then she had started talking about herself. Rosa grew up in East LA, which had a lot of gang activity. Her immediate neighborhood was safe and had a thriving Latino community, but gangs and thugs made life uncertain at times. Some respected the old timers who lived there, some didn't give a crap and did what they wanted. By the time Rosa was eighteen, she had three choices: work at her uncle's bodega, go to the community college or join the military. She joined the military and over the years rose from private to corporal. She fought in Afghanistan first and then was stationed in Iraq to protect the green zone. Afghanistan sounded like utter hell to me. She lost friends in Afghanistan, which she was still dealing with. Iraq was a welcome respite comparatively because she was not really involved in any heavy action.

We had also talked about our love lives. I had had many short-term relationships that never really panned out. I admitted that I tended to more interested in the budding romance than the long haul. She only had two serious boyfriends, one back in East LA who cheated on her, and one in Iraq who ended up getting stationed in Asia. The rest were flings. She told me she was starting to fall in love with the guy in Iraq, but he was suddenly yanked from her. That was military life. It wasn't all serious. We'd also talked about food and movies and music. None of which we had at the moment, but she could sing and sung a lonely sounding song in Spanish. After that part of the ride together, we became close; two strangers sharing their lives as civilization fell apart around us.

With practice over, I make the suggestion we spend the night. There were trees we could camp under, toilets and one of those park stand-up barbeques we could use to heat up a couple cans of beans.

Before sunset we cook the beans on the barbecue, making a fire using twigs and fallen branches Rosa cut into size with the ax. The plates come in handy and we use the remaining crackers to scoop up the beans. With the tents set up we kill the evening by sitting in the darkness talking. We don't want to draw attention so there's no fire at night.

"So what do you think caused all this?" Alex asks.

"I'm betting this is just the start of a full-scale alien invasion." Alvie's always been a bit of a conspiracy theorist. "You know, knock the power out, sending us into disarray and confusion. Once we are fighting each other, they land and just mop us up."

"That's heartening." My old sense of sarcasm is coming back.

"It could be the grid like the blackout on the east coast in 2003," Alex offers.

"That does not explain the cars and other things like phones and GPS," Rosa reminds us. "It's more like an EMP, but for something to wipe out power over such a large area it would have to be nukes, and there were no nukes."

"See, it has to be aliens. They probably have some giant EMP gun or something."

"Maybe it's Gaia." I stare into the darkness, ruminating on this thought.

"Who?" Alvie asks.

"The Greek and Roman goddess of Earth. She is Earth personified, she is the ecosystem and all life," Alex explains. I'm impressed.

"Yes, I'm just throwing this out there but with pollution, climate change and the mass extinctions maybe Earth said 'enough' and sent out a pulse from its core shutting everything down." I keep staring into the dark, wondering if the planet is already healing itself.

"It's definitely helping the environment, I'll give you that. But to think Earth consciously turned the power off like someone flipping a switch is a little ridiculous."

"About as ridiculous as aliens," I respond. "Anyway, it was a more a philosophical idea than anything. Could just as well have been massive solar flares."

"Whatever caused it we won't know for a while so there's no point guessing." Rosa stands up. "I'm going to crash. There's only three tents obviously so Ger, if you want you can bunk with me."

I hop up and follow her into the tent a little nervous, heart pumping. She's definitely attractive and we have a bond of sorts but I'm not sure I'm ready for anything right now. I doubt my ability with all the recent stress. As we get inside, she turns to me and says, "Nothing is going to happen, just so you know." I'm relieved. Any other time in my past life I would have been a bit bummed, but right now I just need a friend, not a hookup. "Yes ma'am," I smile.

We lie there with my back to her, and her cuddled up with one arm cradling me. I hold her hand and feel her warmth. I feel myself drifting off. I have no anxiety, just her warm embrace.

DAY 7

Morning. I'm alone in the tent, the light glowing orange through the nylon. I can hear Rosa and the others talking outside. I slept the best sleep I've had in a long time, even before things went to shit. Yawning, I crawl out of the tent.

"Morning, sunshine." Alvie gives me a knowing look and smirks.

"Are you sure that's what you heard?" Rosa addresses them.

"Yeah, we stayed up a bit after you two went to bed," answers Alex. "It definitely sounded like an engine, like a car or something."

"No headlights, though," Alvie adds. "No lights at all, and it wasn't too close."

"I don't like it. We better get moving." Rosa looks at me. "Can you take the tent down while I check the weapons and ammo?"

"Sure thing." Yesterday I would have been stressed about this, but this morning I feel oddly calm.

Packed up, we push the truck to a start and hop in. This time it is Rosa and I in the bed. She is quiet, an intense pensive gaze on the road behind. Occasionally she raises her rifle and sweeps the area with the scope. I pull out the phone and start calling to codes again. Still nothing. Still not much to look at but the landscape starts to change from corn to other fields, mainly wheat from what I can tell.

As the sun gets low, we pull off the road into a turnout and start setting up camp. Rosa has donned her full military gear and hands Alvie and I our guns. She's still pensive, and I catch her scanning the horizon often until the sun sets and darkness crawls across the landscape.

We have one packet of hot dogs and some crushed cereal for dinner. No one is interested in the canned beets, but if we don't find a place to restock that will be tomorrow's meal. We light a small fire to enjoy the luxury of cooked hot dog, impaling them on sticks and holding them over the fire. Alex's stick catches on fire and we laugh as he tries desperately to salvage his hot dog. Dogs eaten, we pass the box of cereal around and munch on that, while discussing random topics like movies we saw recently and whether we liked them or not and why.

I hear something over the fire and talk, a rustling of some kind. "Shhh!" Rosa puts her finger to her lips and we all go instantly quiet and look around. I grab my gun from the ground next to me and sit up to a kneeling position. The rest stand and instinctively spread a few feet away from each other. The rustling gets louder and we can make out three shadows approaching. I make sure my safety is off on my gun and point it in the direction of the oncoming shades. As they enter the dim light of the fire, I see it's the same three rough rednecks from the diner. They have rifles and a shotgun. Redcap's rifle looks similar to Rosa's.

"Well, if it ain't our friends from the diner," Redcap greets.

"How did you find us and why are you here?" Alvie demands.

"Well, see, once we saw you speed though the truck stop we decided we could use another vehicle. You know, something that can haul more than we can fit in the old Buick's trunk."

"Yeah, we've been tracking you," the man next to Redcap offers with a grin sparse of teeth. "Weren't hard."

"Anyway, we'll be taking your truck and your guns and moving on. You can get continue with your little camping party." Redcap stares coldly at Alvie.

"Drop your guns and go before I light you up." Rosa raises her gun and aims directly at Redcap.

"I was wondering when my little soldier girl was going to pipe up." Redcap smirks. "Well boys…"

I hear a trigger being pulled before the bang of the gun. I close my eyes, pull my trigger and wave the gun back and forth like an errant garden hose on full blast. I barely hear the other shots over my leaping beast. Eventually all is silent other than the click, click, click of my empty gun. I slowly open my eyes. The air stinks of cordite and copper. Looking around, I'm the only one upright. Everyone is horizontal. I get up dazed and numb and walk over where Alvie lies. Before I get close, I see he's been shot in the face. I fall to my knees and weep. I'm hollowed out. A pit of loss and despair. Alvie was more than a cousin, he was a best friend. He thought of me first when things started going to hell. He was like the older brother I looked to when I needed one. He was always there. Now he's gone from all that to a memory in thirty seconds. I feel lost, cast upon the desert, aimless.

I hear movement and moaning. Looking around I see Rosa is still alive. She is sitting upright holding her chest. I wipe my tears away and go to her. On my way I see Alex lying face down with several shots to his back. He must have tried to run.

"Are you okay? Have you been hit?"

"Yeah, I've been hit." Rosa responds grumpily. "Vest stopped the bullets but it still hurts like a punta. I think some of my ribs are broken." She says the last bit almost to herself. "How are the others?"

"Dead." I choke out the word.

"Oh, Ger I'm so sorry."

I just nod.

There are more sounds, someone crawling. Turning around I see Redcap trying to crawl away, his leg shattered and bleeding. I reach down to Rosa and pull her handgun from its holster. She looks at me with sadness. She knows. I feel nothing as I walk calmly over to Redcap. He senses me coming and rolls onto his back to face me. His face is wracked with pain and desperation. Nothing.

"Please. This was all a big mistake. We just wanted to scare you into giving us your shit." Nothing.

"Come on man. No one was supposed to get killed but someone jumped the gun." Nothing.

"Look you can leave me here in the middle of nowhere. I don't want to die. Please!" Nothing. I raise the gun, pointing it at his head. *Nothing.*

As the gun kicks, I feel part of part of my soul drifting away on the slight breeze. I walk over to the truck and the pain of loss and anger at the world washes over me again and there's nothing to do but let my eyes bleed out their tears. Rosa crawls over and leans against me. We sit there against the truck as the fire flicks out and leaves us in quiet black. Alone, lost.

I hear a beeping that rouses me out of my stupor. I look around confused. "The phone!" Rosa exclaims. Suddenly alert, I pull it out of my pocket, hit the answer button and raise it to my ear.

"Hello…"

ROADS UNPAVED

BY AMBER BENBOW

DAY 0

A blur of red shot past the right of my peripheral vision. Instinctively, I hit the brakes to avoid the collision. My tires glided, at a slow controlled speed, over the snow packed ice. I was able to correct and meet the pavement again. The red sedan took the ditch, nose first. A pang of regret shot through me as images of a man bloodied or unconscious filled my head. It was the five and a half inches of fresh, unplowed powder that prevented me from stopping. I knew if I did, I wouldn't be able to get going again. Besides, I would have been of marginal help to him and be putting my daughter Sophie at risk. In the back of my mind, I promised to help next time. Now just wasn't a good time.

I cursed work. If they had let me go at two when I asked, when the worst of it started, I would not have been in this mess. Frustration boiled within me. Even leaving at two meant the doubling of my commute.

"Coverage," my boss had said. "We need someone here to field any calls."

It was 6:40 pm by the time we pulled onto our street, an hour and half later than usual. I saw the fat flakes still falling dense as a tropical storm through the windshield. I gunned the little sedan up the slanted driveway, listening to the muffled crunch of snow beneath my tires and bumper. I stepped out of the car into knee deep snow. My skin, red hot from repeated ventures into the snow, protested. I pushed on, reaching for Sophie in the back.

Her face peeked out of her teddy bear snowsuit, her ruddy cheeks and grey eyes sparkling back at me. She was wiggly after having been strapped into her seat for so long. I knew she would be hungry. At eight months old, she was eating easy solids, but I wouldn't have time to make dinner fast enough for her. A bottle should tide her over.

I let the list of endless needs wash over me. There was more to do than time to do it. At least things were better this way. Better for me to be overwhelmed by the chaos of life then be with that two-timing bastard. The least he could have done was tell me about his wife. It was better for everyone that Sophie and I had disappeared.

I lifted her out of the seat, slung her diaper bag over my shoulder, and wearily eyed the fresh snow between where I stood and the front door. My office pants and flats were the wrong choice for today. *Too bad I left my parka and snowshoes at home*, I rolled my eyes, steeling myself. *Like I even own a parka.* Snow against my warm body bit down, digging its jagged teeth into my flesh, invading my socks and shoes. I longed for a sensible pair of winter boots. Generally snow in Minneapolis came in bursts a few inches at a time, leaving time for the streets to be cleared and a modest snowbank to pile up. This was different. This felt desperate.

Carrying Sophie in, I looked at the old oak trees hanging close to the house I was renting. Never once did I break my stride as doing so would prolong the needling pain to my legs and feet. Still, I noticed the beauty of the snow, thick and heavy as it clung to the elderly trees.

"Okay, Sophie, let's get the teapot on and dinner going, then we'll enjoy the blizzard."

I set her down on the shaky front steps, balancing her gingerly while still unearthing my keys from my bag. Succeeding, I opened the door and pressed into the house, carrying Sophie in and dropping our things. Judging by the newly formed drifts of snow around my car, it was clear I wasn't going anywhere tonight and likely not tomorrow either. No work tomorrow meant a smaller paycheck. I sighed, trying not to get too far ahead of myself. I hadn't unzipped Sophie or started to cook.

One thing at a time Dana, one thing at a time.

"Bottle first, hmm?"

Sophie crawled across the floor on the other side of the pen. I stood in the kitchen, hovering menacingly over carrots and onions, hoping to get a quick soup going. The oil snapped and popped over the drone of the radio. The storm was hitting fast and hard.

"Traffic cameras are reporting fifty spinouts on the major highways and six multicar accidents are causing additional delays," the reporter listed off. "Officials are warning commuters not to travel unless absolutely necessary."

I looked up from my chopping to see Sophie clinging to the baby gate. Her cheeks hinted at the red they had been from the cold and fussing. My body was warming up from the hike through the snow and I knew my own cheeks had that same rosy glow. The snow danced outside, thick as ever. I felt good knowing we might have a surprise weekend in the middle of the week.

"Ba?" she said.

"Oh honey, mommy's busy." I chopped through more carrots in a few strokes. "In a little bit we can--"

I froze. The kitchen went dark. The radio silent. The popping of the onions in the oil slowed.

There wasn't a word left in my throat.

I took a ragged breath and wrapped my face into the crook of my arm. I stood there hunched over the island, my hair in the vegetables, devising my next steps. I laughed dryly. Everything felt stack against me.

An unsure whimper that ramped up into a wail.

"It's okay, baby. It's okay." I said, ducking my fingers under water and wiping them on a towel.

I felt my way to the gate as my eyes had not adjusted to sudden change in illumination. There I met her outstretched hands. I tucked her onto my hip where she clutched my shirt. Her whimpering calmed. Having me close and mumbling sweet reassurances to her was enough.

"It's okay, mommy needs to find a flashlight or a candle...or something." I reached for my pocket, tapping my butt to confirm the pocket was empty. The kitchen was washed in grays and blues. My eyes hadn't adjusted enough to see where something as small as my phone might be. Instead, I saw the general outline of appliances and the brighter contrast of the kitchen window. I closed my eyes for a moment, trying to remember where I left it.

In my bag.

I crossed the room in a couple of quick strides to pull my phone. "Hold on a moment," I said to Sophie, setting her down on the floor. Perturbed, she let her thoughts be known.

I thumbed the phone on, its bright screen providing wanted light in the darkness. There was a text waiting.

Is your power out too? My best friend Kaylan asked.

My sister May responded, *Yeah, we're down. Do you think it was the ice?*

I read the group text and started to type in a few letters before Sophie pulled on my jeans. "Hang on, I'm getting something." I flick the top menu down and snap the flashlight on.

"That's better. Now let's see if we can find something a little more 'hands-free'." I said, then stuffed my phone in my mouth. I lifted her up and curled her close.

"Here, can you hold this?" I hand her my phone, which she puts directly into her mouth too. "Hold it straight, please."

I found five candle sticks, each a different color. They aren't mine and I was curious who would need one of each color and if that meant the previous person was eclectic or ominous.

I traded Sophie two candlesticks for my phone. She definitely got the better end of the deal.

"To the kitchen!" We spun around and I raspberried her. She shrieked in delight, dropping a candle.

I scanned the kitchen. I was unwilling to search the house on the off chance someone left a candelabra for the occasional power outage. In a drawer, was a lighter.

Thankfully the recycling bin yielded an empty wine bottle. Lighting one of the candles, I screwed it into the top of the bottle. I tried to twist out the tension in my shoulder while I watched the wax drip at a precarious 45 degree angle onto the countertop. The fit wasn't quite snug enough.

I snapped a picture, sending it to Kaylan and May. *Wax scrapes up, right?*

They would know from my picture that the power was down for me too.

I stuck a plastic plate under the wine bottle to protect the counters.

Now what? I scanned the kitchen. The pot of would-be-soup was quiet. "What doesn't need to be heated, Sophie?" I pushed boxes of noodles to the back of the cupboard. I set the candle and its plate on the floor, peering between the packages.

"Fig Newtons and room temperature tikka masala sound okay to you?" Sophie banged two blocks together in response.

I couldn't stomach the tikka masala without the rice, so I spread it thinly across tortillas convincing myself that it was an exotic taco. Sophie refused it, preferring chunks of the fig newtons to gum up.

In less than an hour, the temperature drop was perceptible. "Brrrr," I said in my silly voice. No one was fooled, not even Sophia.

I checked online to see when the power would be back. They offered a semi-reasonable three hours given the conditions. The chatter online was curious, with neighbors checking in on each other and to see how far the outage was. There was no need for me to call the power company myself or drain my battery, so I tapped the lock button on my phone.

I laid Sophie across her changing pad, undoing her snaps. She began to roll away when the cold hit her skin.

"Shh, shhh, honey. It's okay." With my mad karate-mom skills, I changed her and then wrestled her into her PJs. She was protesting when I tried to point her foot into the footie.

I estimated that the ambient temperature was about sixty-five degrees and it was coming down. Rapidly.

It's incredible how much you can hear when the entire house is powered down. From across the street I heard voices calling to each other. Nothing distinct, but enough to recognize the edge of concern beneath them. I realized there was no humming fridge, no furnace kicking on, no fan over the oven, nor the dim, distant hum of lights. The sounds of the night intruded like a muffled TV.

Still the snow kept on.

By 8:00 pm there was still no update to the power ETA. It was still reading three hours. I let out a deep sigh, willing myself to relax. Even four hours wouldn't be too bad. Everything would work out.

When I crept into Sophie's room, I estimated it was now about fifty-eight degrees in the house. I stroked her cheek which was flushed from wearing two jumpers. Dread ate at my belly, twisting it. It felt like black oil curling through me. I didn't know how to protect her. I tucked the blanket in tight around her. Tonight, I was more afraid of the cold then SIDs.

Unable to think of another thing to do, I dragged an extra comforter onto my bed and went to sleep early. I wore a pair of leggings, a sports top, fitted t-shirt, sweatshirt and my thickest socks. Under the comforter it wasn't so bad. Checking on Sophia for the 50th time wasn't going to make her more comfortable nor ease my mind. I plugged my phone in and the lack of acknowledgement made me snort. *Right, like camping.*

I woke up to my whole body feeling cold and tingly. My breath came steaming out in hot curls. The room was as dark with no glow from the streetlights impeding the gray.

I clicked my phone. It was 11:52 pm, perhaps it was down to the low fifties now. I felt uncomfortably chilled as soon as I left the covers. I skittered to Sophie's room where she slept soundly in her crib. I brushed a hand over her cheek to check her temperature again. She felt cold to the touch, but the back of her head radiated heat. I slipped two fingers down the back of her jumper and she felt comfortable. A shiver ran through me as the cold penetrated my layers. My breath picked up a hitch and I pressed my clenched fisted into my heart. *How long until she is too cold? What if I laid her down for the last time and didn't know it?* Acid rose up in my throat and I choked it down.

Crawling back into bed, desperate now, I unplugged my phone and started scrolling. There was an update on the power company's site stating that they had "encountered some unforeseen difficulties in restoring power". My breath hitched up a notch--that was about an hour ago. We were approaching six hours without electricity and the temperature was dipping fast. Come morning would likely be 34 degrees inside—almost as cold as outside.

My mind began to churn. I went back to Sophia's crib and scooped her up. I tucked her into bed with me. With her double jumpers and all the layers on my bed, I was anxious she might be too warm, but this made me feel safest. I was doing the most I could to protect her and prevent her from slipping away from me in the middle of the night. She barely stirred, sucking on her tongue in her sleep, and curling into my embrace.

Alertness hung at the edges of my sleep. There was no rest.

DAY 1

Sophie's happy chirps woke me. She was trying to climb on me since I must have looked like a good mountain to summit. Out the window I saw the wind drifting snow across the yard. Plows rumbled down the street a few blocks away. We were snowed in and I stretched out, a little relieved. My room felt comfortable, given our layers, but as soon as I opened the bedroom door a wall of cold came crashing in like the tide. The heat bubble burst, letting our accumulated body heat escape into the empty house.

Last night's panic was a warmup drill for the lightening of white hot adrenaline that coursed through me. I paced back and forth, considering my options and wiping my now damp palms on my leggings.

I went back to my phone, it's battery flashing red. I saw several texts about the situation from Kaylan and May.

Kaylan: *Still no power, what about you?*

May: *We are going to fire up the generator if you can get here.*

Kaylan: *Got to wait for the plows to come through and then we might venture out. My battery's almost dead.*

May: *Okay, try to let us know if you can. We'll expect you both no matter what.*

I tapped in a reply. *Same on battery and plows. Turning off phone for now. See you when I can.*

Before turning off my phone, I sent my boss a quick text too. *We're snowed in. Should be in tomorrow.*

Sophie crawled up to me, pulling herself up using my shirt. I looked at her, "My God, what am I going to feed you?" She gurgled a confident reply.

Turns out diaper changes are significantly easier when your child is not trying to escape: your cold hands, the cold air, or the cold wipe. In fact, all of these factors combined will result in poop on the changing cover. Following this excursion in acrobatics, I focused, single handedly on the task of feeding my child. Her food was easy as it was a little bit of powdered cereal mixed with formula.

Done.

Now for me?

Eggs? No.

Oatmeal? No.

Pancakes? No.

Noodles? No.

Sandwiches for everyone! I felt like I had won a million dollars. Not really, but it's hard to feel bad about your life when you are eating PB&J. Or maybe it was the opposite, I always felt bad about my life when I was eating PB&J. I ate with renewed vigor.

I packed the diaper bag, grabbed my charger, and bundled Sophie up. She seemed happy to be in her oversized bear snowsuit for once. Previously she tried to fight her way out of it, but now it seemed like a welcome accessory to her. I smiled down at her. How cute she was with her round baby cheeks looking like an anime teddy bear. I wanted to squeeze her tightly to my body, so instead I reached for my phone to take a picture. I pulled it from my pocket and double tapped it's black screen. *Modern life is a series of habits,* I realized, stuffing the useless brick into my back pocket. *And not all of them good.* I loaded the diaper bag and carrier into the car.

Driving in snow is similar to navigating a boat with an oversized motor through a pond. It's about applying the right amount of pressure when needed, coasting the rest of the way, and making sure you stay out of the weeds. The weeds, in this case, are mounds of snow drifts left by the plows.

Those of course, need a running head start for anything smaller than a pickup to make it through.

But I made it to May and Jordan's. This was the highlight, not of my day, but my week. Here was a place with all the modern conveniences. They had their furnace running, though well below capacity, and the fridge was still humming. The first thing I did after we arrived was plug my phone in. Sophie played with her two year old cousin Aiden on the carpet in the living room.

"This has been one hell of an adventure," I vented to my sister. She handed me a cup of hot cocoa which I wrapped my fingers around soaking in the heat. "How much longer do you think it will be?"

May shrugged, sipping her own hot cocoa. "Probably by this afternoon. Though, if Kaylan doesn't get here soon, I think one of us should go out and look for her."

"You haven't heard anything either?"

May shook her head. Jordan looked up from his sudoku, brows furrowed. "How long has it been?" he asked.

"A few hours. She said she was snowed in."

After a few more hours, the generator cycling on a few times, it became clear that Sophie and I will have to leave. My obsessive checking online hadn't revealed a miraculous power restoration. At this point, I wonder how long it will be before it comes back.

"You don't need to leave," my sister says. "It may not be comfortable sleeping on the floor but we have comforters to throw down and it sure beats sleeping in a cold house alone."

"Thank you," I agree, too quickly and hug her. I feel like there is no where else for me to go and I thank God that I have somewhere safe for Sophie.

I'm out of diapers though.

Tomorrow, everything will be back to normal.

DAY 5

The announcement reads:

> *We regret that we are not able to be more informative at this time, but residents will not see the restoration of power for at least several more days. Temporary shelters have been established at the following locations: community centers, malls, arenas, and other designated community relief zones. Please check with your local authorities for more information. We urge residents to ration generator use to conserve fuel.*

And with one simple, yet vague post (can it be considered vague-booking if you're a power company?), all hell broke loose. The line for the gas station stretched two and a half blocks long. People were coming to fuel up not their vehicles but to get additional gas for their generators, those who were smart enough to have them anyways.

Though I was still anxious I was less afraid than the first night alone. Now I have community, those to gather around me. One to stand in line for gas, one to gather fallen branches for the fireplace, one to mind the children, and one to spare. This must be what life was like a hundred years ago. We were closer, more connected. We relied on each other for survival and right now I can feel it more than anything.

This doesn't feel so bad. I can live with this.

DAY 43

I sat my gas can next to the rear wheel of the pickup and carefully fed the first tube into the tank. Then I made sure it was secure to the gas can. I looked around quickly, making sure no one would come to scare me off. This was my fourth try of the day, all of the gas tanks had been empty. I fished out the smaller tube from my pocket and a rag to seal them. Then I blew as hard as I could until the gas started to flow into the can.

"What the hell are you doing?"

The sharp voice made the hair on my neck stand. Hunger and apathy have numbed me. I gripped the tube tighter.

"It's been three weeks, Tyler. You're either with us, or you get out of our way." Jordan stands behind me, his pistol drawn.

THE NIGHT THAT CHANGED EVERYTHING

BY SHAUN CURTIS

DAY 0

"What part of 'stay calm', was so damn hard to understand?" I said in a stern voice to the half dozen people around me. Just because the power goes outs does not mean we need to panic. Besides, the power goes out all the time in places, including hospitals. As a matter of fact, if you have to be anywhere when the power does go out, a hospital is probably one of better places to be. You see, all hospitals have back-up generators to keep all the patients safe in case of a power loss event. Wouldn't look very good if all those sick and injured were to die on us, now would it?

I'm sure the darkness in the room seemed to last forever to some of the surgical team. When you are in the middle of an operation, even the slightest hick-up can become a disaster. For this very reason we are all trained to keep our cool. It's what separates us from the rest of the world. Shit happens and that is just a fact of life. How you deal with it is a true test of our character. Some people handle it, some rely on others to handle it, and the rest, well, they just lose their minds and panic. The sooner you get the people who panic under control, the sooner things can return to normal, or at least what resembles normal.

The team of professionals working with me were the best, or so I believed. The true way to find out who is the best is to experience the worst. Having the power go out shouldn't have been one of those, 'worse', moments. Unless that is, if the power never comes back on. I never for a second thought that would be the case. Boy was I ever mistaken.

"Ladies and gentlemen, we are all professionals here." I said to the team, who up until this very moment were doing a bang-up job with this surgery.

"As you can all see, we have lost power. It happens. There is no need to panic, let's just keep our heads on our shoulders and continue what we were doing."

One of the surgical nurses, I think her name was Amy, looked over to me and said,

"Doctor Miller, we should have some headlamps under the I.V. storage cabinets. Who should I give them to?"

"Myself, one to Dr. Jones, our anesthesiologist, followed by the head surgical nurse, Tameron, and my surgical intern, Dr. Baker. After that spread them out as you see fit."

Amy immediately retrieved the equipment and dolled it out as instructed. It turned out, we all got equipped with battery powered headlamps. While this is all taking place, I hear my intern calling me.

"Dr. Miller, we have a bleeder." I look over to him.

"Well of course we do, cause why not!" It turns out, while this was a simple appendectomy, when the lights went out, something nicked an artery.

"Nurse, Hemostat please. Dr. Baker, grab a large Kelly (devise used to clamp large vessels and tissue), and help me get ahold of this bleeder before this routine surgery becomes anything but."

We make fast work of the bleed and refocus on the task at hand, the appendectomy. All this takes place in a matter of minutes. In those precious minutes, the lights blink on, go off and then stay on.

"Ok everyone, the power is back, at least for now. Given the power has flickered on and off multiple times, we are probably on back-up power. Let's close up this patient before something else happens." You could almost feel tension in the air dissipate the moment the power returned. My team and I finished the job at hand, with me turning the closing over to my intern, Dr. Baker.

As I watched him stitching up the patient, I shouted out some instructions to the rest of my staff as to what to do and told my head surgical nurse Mrs. Harper that I am going to find out what happened and if I was needed anywhere. Nurse Harper nodded and I left the surgical unit to wash up and put on some new scrubs.

A person might not think a temporary blackout would or could cause such chaos, let me tell you, that person would be wrong. In complete darkness, the simple act of walking becomes a fight for survival in a hospital environment. Just think about it for a second, you have gurneys and wheelchairs in the halls, hell, there are even patients walking around trying to recover with friends and family. Not to mention children of guests, chairs and medical carts. The afore mentioned are just a few things you have to contend with. When it goes from a well-lit hospital to a dark maze of passages and corners filled with people and other obstacles, well, to put it mildly it's like the blind leading the blind. Every step has to be planned if that's possible. That is why there are emergency lights everywhere that come on automatically when the power goes off. Only their batteries don't last forever.

Fortunately, at the moment, with generators kicking in, all the lights were on.

Working my way down the hall, I was amazed at the mess that was created in the relatively short period of time that the power was down. I couldn't help but think what might happen if the power is not restored before the generators run out of fuel. What happens then would be nothing short of a practice in patience, determination, and fortitude – and a lot of luck.

DAY 0 [+1 HOUR]

As I walked the halls of the hospitals helping out those I could, I realized I had better see how many supervisors were in the building. Knowing there had to be some kind of protocols for these situations I decided now was a good time to see what those protocols might be. As a surgeon, we are trained to expect the worst and be thankful for the best. I took this advice and applied it to all aspects of my life.

As I made my way toward the administration wing of the hospital, a middle-aged man walked down the hall in a manner that can only be described as lost.

"Sir, Sir, may I help you find someone or assist you in finding someplace here in the hospital?"

The man looks at me immediately and says, "Yes you may as a matter of fact." The change in demeaner from looking lost to having all his faculties about him took me back for a second.

Gathering myself I say, "Tell me what I can help you with then."

He looked at me and said, "Have you heard any radio's or cell phones ringing -- in fact, anything we normally consider background noise and tend to tune them out?"

His question set me back. I had been so wrapped up in what I was doing, I failed to notice anything else. I took a moment to tune into my surroundings.

"I'm sorry, I've seemed to have forgotten my manners. My name is Dr. Jack Miller, I am a surgeon here at the hospital."

I hold out my hand to shake and he extends his arm and says, "It's nice to meet you Jack, my name is Sidney, Sidney Daniels."

With the nice to meet you and other formalities out of the way we return to the original question at hand.

"Now that you mention it Sidney, I don't hear anything more that the chattering of people and shuffling of equipment." Nodding his head, he looks to me.

"I guess it's just a by-product of my career in intelligence that I happen to notice things that seem out of the ordinary. In today's society, it's next to impossible to find a quiet place to think. There is always something going on everywhere, all the time, 24-7-365."

I stand there and think for a moment and realize he is one hundred percent correct, there really is a lot going on around us all the time.

"Damn Sidney, your right. Now that I think of it there really is nowhere truly quiet —especially at my house with two kids under five."

The humor was short-lived. We both stood there taking it all in. The lack of background noise was staggering. Sure, there were noises from inside the hospital and those in it, noises customary to such a place. But nothing from outside.

"Jack, can you see if you can make a phone call? Cell or land line if you can."

Curious, I walked over to a nurse's station and picked up the phone, nothing. No dial tone. I reached for my cellphone, bring it out of sleep mode, bring up the contacts list and tap dial. Again, nothing at all, not even a carrier message telling me that all the circuits are busy and to try again later, absolutely nothing. I turn to Sidney and shake my head.

"There is nothing on either of the phones." Sidney looks at me.

"Let's not jump to conclusions just yet. Those things may just be affected by the power loss and will return when it comes back on." I nod my head and see the logic in that statement.

"How can we find out how widespread the outage is?"

"Internet!" We both say. As fast as this comes to our minds it leaves just as quickly.

"If your local provider has lost their power, we won't have service here." I say this and no sooner than I do Sidney says, "Satellite Phones, do you know anyone that might have one?" I look at him.

"Satellite, cell, what's the difference?" Sidney lets a little chuckle out.

"I can see where people might confuse the two. However, satellite phones send their signal up to a satellite in space and then back down to the other phone."

"So essentially, as long as the battery in the phone is charged and the satellite hasn't fallen from the sky it should work, yes?"

Sidney nods his head. "Basically, yes, in a nutshell."

"This is a hospital, not a military installation. I can't think of anyone on staff who would need one." I thought a minute more. "There are two possibilities. There is a slim chance Dr. Michaels, our medical director, might have one. He works with some outreach projects around the world – many in areas where there are no utilities to speak of.

"The other possibility would be if we happen to have any patients, such as yourself, who might have need of one – such as a military or government official. In either case, Dr. Michaels should be able to help us."

"Where is his office?"

"Follow me."

We hadn't made it more than twenty-five feet down the hall when, 'Blackness'. This time, it was complete. Not even the emergency lights came on. The only illumination came from leds on various pieces of equipment operating on battery power.

"Well of course this would happen, because why not?" I said, standing next to Sidney, or at least I hope I am still next to him. The darkness was so complete I swear you couldn't see your hand in front of your face.

"Sidney? You still here?" As panic once again began to ensue, I could hear people running into things and the toppling of carts, and people crying.

"Sidney!"

"Yes Jack, I am here. You sound like you're just off to my left. Hold still, I'll make my way over to you

He signaled his arrival by tapping me on my shoulder. "Let's get against a wall and get a sense of where we are."

I did not recall any equipment or carts along the wall in the hall we were in. I took a few careful steps to my right, my arm outstretched, feeling for the way. Sidney kept his hand on my shoulder, following my movement. Shortly, we found ourselves leaning against the wall.

"What the hell happened now"?" I asked, agitated the world was not cooperating.

In his inherently calm demeaner Sidney replied, "I think we need to find our way to the generator room."

While I am intelligent, hell I made it through med school and became a surgeon after all, my expertise is not all-encompassing. I am a fixer of bodies, human bodies, not mechanical things.

"What exactly are we going to do in the generator room, if I may be so bold?"

"At this moment we have no power." He says. "As far as I know the only thing that is capable of making power are the generators. So, if we find the generators than we might have a chance of regaining power. Does that sound about right?"

"The hospital engineer, no doubt, is already there and working on it." I replied. "We have a large staff for just that purpose."

"The fact the emergency lights failed to come on, tells me something else may be going on. The best place to start finding out why is the generator room."

As much as I hated to admit it, he had an excellent point. "The question now becomes, where in the hell are we and where the hell is the generator room from here?"

"Well doc, this is your hospital." I smile, which seems silly given no one is able to see me do it in the dark.

"Indeed, it is… Indeed, it is…" I say.

DAY 0 [+2 HOURS]

As Sidney and I went off in search of the generator room, I tried to think of all the times I helped my friends or family work on their vehicles. My hope was there was an easy fix for the generator that might help bring it online again and stay that way.

The penlight I had on me worked just well enough to help us find our way to the maintenance area of the hospital. My true hope was that we would get there to find the maintenance crew hard at the problem.

Ha, no such luck.

We found our way downstairs to the power room. Everything was dark. Worse, everything was quiet.

"Hello," I shouted upon entering, knowing the absence of light probably meant the absence of people. I tried anyway. "Anyone in here?"

The silence was deafening.

There was still some heat in the room from when the generator was running but no ear-piercing sound of the massive caterpillar engines that the hospital uses for their back-up power. Or the clank clank of someone working to fix the problem.

"Well that's just great! Darker than a well diggers ass in here doc." Sidney says to me.

"You know Sidney, I haven't had a lot of time around diesel motors but, is that strong smell always accompanied with these beasts?" I shine my pen light around the room and see the behemoth engines that should be screaming right now, supplying the hospital with the power it needs to continue to function normally. Instead, they are sitting here as quiet as grizzlies in hibernation.

We continue to scan the room when Sidney all of the sudden commands,

"Doc, stop."

I immediately hold still, anticipating the worst.

"What's the matter?" "Move your light a bit to your right."

I do.

"Well I think I see why the generators are not running, and unfortunately I think I see why the diesel fuel smell is so strong."

As my light shined across the floor of the room, something on the floor reflected back. Initially, it appeared to be a puddle of water on the floor of the room. We both walk towards the semi-flooded area adjacent the center of the three massive motors, the increasing stench cluing us in as to what we found.

When we get there, Sidney bent down, put a finger in the pool and brought it back to his nose, confirming what we suspected.

"Diesel fuel." He said.

We continue our scan of the room, walking around the machines when I noticed a hole in one of the doors encasing the motors. "What do you think did that?" I asked Sidney. On the upper portion of the inspection door is a hole easily the size of my head. The thin metal sounding the hole is jagged and flaring outward as if something had punched a hole in it, from the inside

As Sidney and I stand there trying to figure out what this means he called out, "Boom."

"What exactly do you mean by, 'Boom'?"

"Well, it looks like the generator had a catastrophic failure." We both look up at the hole in the machine again.

"So, you think something like a connecting rod broke and the piston head went through the side?" "So, you are not just a just a fixer of people?" Sidney replied, with a smile in his voice.

"My dad was a mechanic all his life and I picked up a few things here and there." We panned the light back around to the puddle of fuel. I then followed the puddle to what I hoped was the source.

"I may not be a mechanic. However, I know of not a single internal combustion engine that can function without a fuel supply." I said. "I don't want to know, do I?"

I turn the flashlight toward what I am assumed to be the fuel tank centrally located between the generators.,

"If you follow the exit of whatever broke and shot through the generator housing and follow it's trajectory it goes towards the fuel tank.

I fixed the light on a dark spot on the tank. "Now, you see that hole in the tank?" This time, the jagged edges around the perfectly round hole are pointing inward.

"That would be the hole that is no longer leaking fuel that you are referring to?"

"That would be the one. It also accounts for the strong smell of fuel oil."

"Well if that's not just a pile of crap wrapped up in a shiny package."

"That's one way to put it." I replied.

We stand there for a few more moments, contemplating what to do next.

"Sidney, you were saying something about satellite phones?"

"Yes, as it pertains to the power outage, why?"

I don't say anything for a moment as I contemplated.

"As this appears to be a dead end, I say we try to locate a sat-phone on our way to the air ambulance office on the upper level." This puts a bit of a confused look on Sidney's face.

"Why the a do we need a helicopter?" he asks.

"I'm glad you asked. I would very much like to see just how far this blackout reaches. In the air we can see most of the city."

We head out toward the stairwell on the opposite side of where we came in. As we opened the door, we discover the emergency lights are still functioning.

"When this is all over, I will have to check into why all the emergency flood lights in the hospital except these aren't functioning."

We start our ascent up the stairwell when Sidney asked, "Do you think the pilots might have a sat phone?"

"Never thought of that. However, if anyone is likely to have one it would be them. Good thinking. Even if they don't, their radios have a much longer range – especially when in the air."

DAY 0 [+3.5 HOURS]

We walked up the stairs for what seemed like forever, even though it's only a six-story building. "Ok, note to self, more time on the stair stepper at the gym." I said. Sidney laughed.

"Come on doc, it's only six flights of stairs."

As we get climb the last set of stairs to the roof access, we stop as there is a lock requiring a code to access the roof. "I forgot about the door having a lock. And without power . . ."

"Well, this may pose a slight problem."

We both just stare at the dark keypad in front of us in defeat.

"When an inbound bird is on its way, this door is already open by the attending emergency response crew. If no one, for some reason or another is not here by the time the crew lands, the crew can open it via a bump bar from the outside in order to gain access to the hospital. This helps to avoid any precious time that might be wasted." I told Sidney.

"Fat lot of good that does us on this side of the door."

"We need to come up with another way out there."

"Good point."

Pondering how we are going to get through the door I walked up to it and pushed, it opens.

"Well, I feel like a real genius now. Electronic lock with no power can't lock I guess." Sidney shakes his head.

"Alright doc, you got me there. I should have thought about the fact that a magnetic lock would need power to stay shut." I told him we will call it even and we head out to the landing pad.

In front of us we could see the outline of the air ambulance in all its glory, illuminated only by the moon.

I took a moment to look up at the star-filled sky. "I had no idea there were so many stars!" I remarked to Sidney. "Normally you can't see many with the light noise from the city." Sidney nodded in agreement.

"I always wanted to learn to fly one of these things." I told Sidney as we walked around the copter heading to the crew quarters on the opposite side of the roof. When we arrive, I knocked on the door. The door opened and out stepped a bleary-eyed crew member.

"Can I help you?" I heard these crews work long hard hours at time, but this guy looked as though he just came back from a sleep depravation study.

"I sure hope so." I said. Similar to a cold fluorescent light coming to life, a look of 'what's wrong with this picture' came over his face.

"Hey, why is it so dark out here, other than the fact that it is night and all?" The crew member asks.

"Have you and your crew been asleep the last couple of hours?" Sidney asked.

"Yes, as a matter of fact we have been, why, what's happened?"

I introduced myself and Sidney and told him a short version of the events plaguing the hospital in the last few hours. He told me his name was Steve and that he and his crew just returned from a major pile-up on the tollway. That accident took them most of the night shuttling people back and forth from accident scene to the hospital.

"So, while we were sleeping, the hospital, neighborhood, maybe even the city has lost power?"

Sidney and I both nodded.

"Yep, that sounds about right as far as we can determine." Just then Sidney jumped in.

"The aforementioned series of events is why we are here now."

Steve looked at Sidney and asked "What can we help you with then?" Just as he finished asking his question another person came to the door.

"What's going on? I could really use a few more ZZZZ's if possible."

Steve opened the door wider and introduced us to another of his crew.

"Jack, this is Madison, and... sorry sir I don't remember getting your name." He pointed at Sidney..

Sidney laughed. "I'm sorry, my name is Sidney Daniels. It's nice to meet you both. Is it just you two or are there any other crew members?"

Steve looked past Madison and then at her. "Have you seen George?"

"Same place and in the same position as he passed out when we got back." They both start to laugh, then Steve asked Madison,

"Did he at least get out of his flight suite this time?" Madison looked over to Steve and shook her head.

"I am sure there is a very good story here to be had, however, can you tell us from the air?" I asked.

Steve and Madison asked simultaneously, "From the air?"

I looked at Steve, then Madison. "I am sure you're very tired. If there were any other way, believe me, I would use it. However, as it is right now, we have no power, the generators are not functioning, and we have no way of communicating with anyone outside this immediate area. This is why we need your help."

They both looked at us dumfounded.

I continued. "First, see if you can contact air traffic control. If I'm right, you will find you can't."

Steve stared at me for a moment, then walked over to the radio control board. He grabbed the microphone and flipped a switch. "Control, this is NCX031, come in please."

Silence. "Control, this is NCX031, come in please." The only sound was static.

Now Steve wore a very concerned look. He fiddled with a dial on the control panel. "This ix NCX031, we have a mayday. Please respond." He repeated the process several more times.

"This can't be happening," he commented. "At any time, there are fifty or more aircraft in the area that should be able to hear my call. I even tried the commercial airline bands. Nothing."

Madison asked, "So how can we help?"

I looked at Sidney and he gave me a 'go ahead' look, so I did. "We would like you to take us up to see how far this black-out reaches. This may give us an idea just what we are dealing with. It may also allow us to extend our radio reach."

Sidney spoke up. "Do you have a sat phone by any chance?"

Steve paused, "Yes we do, why?"

DAY 0 [+4.5 HOURS]

We got into the flight crew's quarters and Steve yelled out, "George, get your lazy ass out of that rack, we have shit to do."

From a back room somewhere we heard, "Go to hell, I never heard the 'get to work' bell go ding-ding. My ugly ass needs as much beauty sleep as I can, don't want to put the patients into shock when they see me, we are supposed to save them, not kill them."

Madison and Steve nodded while Sidney and I laughed.

"Hey, who you got out there with you?"

"Get out here and see for yourself," Madison replied. "And make it snappy, we really do have something to do, so chop-chop." From the back room we hear movement, some mumbling that sounds something a cry of pain

"Who the hell left their boots in the middle of the floor?"

"Those would be your boots, you moron." Steve answered, "Madison and I already have ours on."

The back room was quiet for a second. "Oh, that makes sense."

George came out to the main room and Steve made introductions, telling George the story. We made plans on how to fly without permission from ATC (air traffic control)

and no way of communicating with any other air traffic in the area.

We came up with a game plan and preparations were made. The pilot, Steve, headed out to make preparations to fly while George the flight paramedic and Madison, the flight nurse, thought of things we might need just in case.

"You know Sidney, I really hope we are both wrong and this is just a local issue."

Sidney turns to me, nodding. "You and me both Doc, you and me both."

We heard the rotors of the chopper starting up. *Whap whap whap.* George and Madison came out of the back part of the building all geared up.

Sidney and I started to head out to the helipad, when Madison spoke up.

"Wait a minute. If the power is out, we will need to have some kind of beacon to find the helipad again."

"I think there are some heavy duty lanterns in the supply closet." George said. "Let me check."

He returned a minute later, holding four battery operated lanterns. "As long as the satellites haven't lost power, the GPS will guide us back to he building. These will help mark the landing pad."

We each grabbed one and headed out to the helicopter pad. We spread out and placed one lantern in the pattern of a square, with the landing pad inside. We see Steve giving us the thumbs up, signaling that we are ready to take our little journey

We then made our way to the helicopter, instinctively ducking, even though the rotors were many feet above our heads. A surprising amount of dirt flew up around. Madison opened the door and we loaded up the aircraft and climbed in, putting on the headsets as instructed by Steve. I take the copilot's seat while Sidney sat behind the pilot.

"Ladies and gentlemen, I would like to welcome you to your round trip flight to god only knows where." Steve laughs to himself.

"As you all are aware there is no power. How far this outage goes is what we are going to try to find out. While flying is the easy part, the more difficult and more tricky part is flying without any help from air traffic control. I know they are not available because I have already tried contacting them." Steve looks around and verifies that everyone in the craft are belted in and ready for take-off.

As we lift off the roof of the building Steve came back on the communications line and filled us in on some other aspects of our flight.

"Ok everyone, I need you to all keep your eyes open for not only lights on the ground but lights in the sky. With the power out, anyone left stranded out here flying is going to be looking for the airport or other suitable landing area." We all told Steve we understood and were ready. With a roar, the helicopter slowly rose from the roof. We cleared the hospital and flew northward.

"Hey doc, I just grabbed the direction off the top of my head. I know there is more city out that direction and the next town of any population at all is closer to the north than any other direction. Shall I keep going or do you have any better ideas?"

Shaking my head, I peered out into the darkness. You know, a person can really take for granted the amount of light that we actually use. Have you heard the expression, 'it's so dark I can't see my hand in front of my face?' Well we assume this kind of darkness is only reserved for caves or horror movies and books. It was that kind of dark outside. Inside, the glow of the instrument panel gave us all a ghostly appearance. It was so dark outside I had to ask Steve how in the hell he knows where he is going.

"GPS and FLIR or Forward-Looking-Infrared-Radar. Which helps me see heat as different colors." Steve also goes on to tell me, "As I am very familiar with the area, I know for a fact that there are no structures above six hundred eighty-five feet other than the cluster of radio towers south of town."

"And the FLIR is for?" Steve smiled and turns some dials on what I assume to be the FLIR.

"Ok doc, you see that whitish color just there on the screen?" I look and nod my head.

"Ok, great. That represents a heat signature. Most buildings will be warm for a while yet giving us time to use them as guideposts. Essentially, if I stay at my designated height and stay clear of any objects on the radar, we should be fine."

I did not need the FLIR to see the most obvious sources of heat. There were massive fires in almost every direction.

Madison was the first to notice, "Guys. Do you see any cars moving? I only see a few headlights."

"You're right. I've been so focused on the buildings." I said. "I hadn't paid attention to the roads. . . Steve, take us down a bit and turn on your searchlight. Let's see if we can tell what's happening."

As we descended, we saw an amazing sight. The roads were clogged with cars – none of which were moving. We could see people abandoning their cars and congregating in groups.

We returned to our cruising height when Steve blurted out, "Do you see any planes? To your right, we should see planes coming into the airport. I don't see any.

"That may explain some of the fires we are seeing." He continued. "If the planes lose power, they won't be able to stay in the air long. If they los their electronics, they won't be able to control the aircraft to even try to glide in."

DAY 0 [+6 HOURS]

"Hey Steve?" Sidney said. "Steve!" he shouted. Then he tapped on his shoulder. "Steve, can you hear me?"

Steve pointed up to a set of buttons above his head and made the number two sign with his hands.

"Can you hear me now?"

Steve nods his head and gives a thumbs up.

"I was asking you about the Sat-phone and if it might be on the chopper with us at the moment?"

He nodded. "We keep one onboard in case we need to reach authorities when we are in a remote area... Hey George, will you reach into the equipment locker and grab the Sat-phone for the doc."

George nodded and proceeded to rifle through the locker until he produced the phone.

The paramedic team wanted to go down to the nearest fire to see if they could help. Sidney and I convinced them there may be worse things ahead. We needed to get a better understanding of what is going on, before we leap into help.

Steve continued to fly north while everyone except George continued to look for signs of any type of power.

George closed the gear locker. "Hot-damn. Found it. Now what Steve?"

Steve replied, "I don't know, ask Sidney or the doc."

George turned to Sidney and gave him the phone.

"Thank you, George."

George nodded, then returned to his seat and continued to scan the area below for signs of power. Sidney powered up the Sat-phone and tried to make a call, pressing the earpiece tight against his ear. He tried several numbers.

"Nothing but static. Either this thing is busted, or all the phone systems are down."

Steve started tapping on one of the instruments on the control ahead of him."

"What's wrong?" I ask.

"The damn GPS system isn't working. Either our GPS is down, or the satellite."

With that, everyone pulled out their phones. No one was getting any signal, phone or GPS.

"Rodger that Doc." Steve replied. "There is nothing coming over the radio, either, on any channel."

"Sidney, tell me that you have some good news." I said.

"Sorry Jack, nothing but static!"

"Wait a minute," Steve interjected, "I'm getting something on a commercial band. Let me patch it through."

'THE FOLLOWING IS A BROADCAST FROM THE EMERGENCY BROADCASTING SYSTEM, THIS IS NOT A TEST. THIS MESSAGE WILL REPEAT ITSELF EVERY 10 MINUTES FROM THE END OF THE MESSAGE. AN UNEXPLAINED PHENOMENON HAS CAUSED A WORLDWIDE POWER LOSS, I REPEAT, WORLDWIDE POWER LOSS. AT THIS TIME IT IS UNCLEAR THE EXTENT OF THE DAMAGE OR HOW LONG IT WILL TAKE TO RESTORE POWER. PLEASE REMAIN CALM AND AWAIT FURTHER INFORMATION AND INSTRUCTIONS. FOR NOW PLEASE CONSERVE ALL BATTERIES AND ANY

OTHER GENERATORS, SEEK SHELTER WITH FRIENDS OR FAMILY. STAY TUNED FOR ANNOUNCEMENTS FROM YOUR STATE AND LOCAL GOVERNMENTS AS TO SHELTERS, AND IF NEEDED, FOOD BANKS. AGAIN, THERE HAS BEEN A WORLDWIDE POWER LOSS. PLEASE REMAIN CALM UNTIL MORE IS KNOWN. GOD BLESS YOU AND GOD BLESS THE UNITED STATES OF AMERICA.'

Everyone in the chopper was dumbstruck.
"Well shit." I said.
"Shit is a word doc, maybe not the one I would use in this particular situation, but indeed a word." Steve said. George, Madison, and Sidney looked forward from the rear of the bird and waited for Steve or me to say something.
We didn't utter a word.

A CONNECTED FAMILY

BY ASHLEY LAINO

DAY 94

My family has always been about technology. The phone played with me, the computer taught me, the TV looked after me. As long as it kept me quiet and out of the way, electronics were my open playground. I lost hours, even days behind a screen. I knew everything about my best friend Mark's life, but I've never heard his voice. I knew how to shoot a gun, but I've never fired a real shot. I traveled the world without leaving my bedroom.

But one day, in what felt like a blink of an eye, my family died. The computers wouldn't turn on, the phones lost all life, all power around me was lost. I was an orphan.

No one really knows for sure what happened. I never paid much attention to the news, and now that the power was gone, news had gone from immediate updates at your fingertips to nothing but whispers and rumors these past few weeks. Everyone around here just called what happened "The Incident." Some people claimed it was a solar flare, others insist that was some sort of terrorist attack, all I knew was that was that when I started eighth grade, I was worried about passing Honors English, not skinning a rabbit.

I wrinkled my nose and glared up at my father. His round stomach drooped over his dirty jeans as he clumsily bent down to pick up some wood. Before "The Incident," my father was an accountant or stockbroker, I wasn't actually sure the title, but I knew it had something to do with money. He was a sweaty, soft-handed man, and it was a miracle he has managed to survive this long.

My mother, who at this time was sitting idly by a pot stirring the water inside, might have been attractive at one point, but that time has long since passed. Her blonde hair had grown too long and now hung in greasy strings over the pot. I noticed glimmers of silver were intermingled with the yellow. How long had she'd been graying? Why hadn't I noticed before? People used to say my mother and I looked alike and I took it as a compliment. I can't say that I would feel the same way now.

We may have been blood, but in very other sense of the word we were strangers to one another. We were forced to stick this out together because of some unspoken societal expectations. Honestly though, if we really wanted to help each other, we probably would have been better going our separate ways.

"Awesome job with that rabbit Greg," My father called out startling me, "Where'd you learn to do that?"

"Hunter's Kill!" I called back, and he nodded as if he understood what on Earth I was talking about.

"Hunter's Kill" was a first person shooter where you had to work your way through the levels killing various wildlife. You started with easy prey and worked your way up to bigger game like bears, until the very last level, where you had to kill the most difficult animal of all and that was another hunter. I didn't have a gun like in the game, so I managed to make some makeshift traps to try and catch small prey like rabbits and squirrels. Most of the time they didn't work, so I just grabbed carcassess that hadn't decayed too much on the sides of roads and in nearby forests and prayed we didn't get sick.

I never got to finish the game, but between each level were side games about wilderness survival, one of those levels was about how to skin an animal. I had crushed that level easily. It seems the game taught me well.

I stripped off the last bit of skin and motioned the carcass towards my mother. Grimacing, she picked up the rabbit between her thumb and forefinger and dropped it into the pot. Before "The Incident" my mother was a stay at home mom, whose mothering entailed drinking wine at noon while watching reality TV on the couch. I doubted she ever thought in a million years that she'd be handling a dead rabbit.

My father managed to get a small fire crackling and we placed the rabbit over it. My parents didn't have the slightest idea how to cook raw, hunted animals, so their approach so far has just been to get the meat as warm as possible.

Once the hare was deemed appropriately hot enough, we sat in silence, chewing slowly on the meager scraps the rabbit provided. Suddenly, we heard the old, crunching of tires on gravel.

We stared at each other in silent bewilderment. There were still some cars running, but not many. So many people relied on oil for generators, gas had become a precious commodity. So hearing a car anymore was rare.

Upon reflection, we probably should have run. The car could have belonged to anyone. There were a lot of looters roaming around these days looking for camps and houses to raid. In fact, our house had been ransacked right after "The Incident." My father had unsuccessfully driven us around the neighborhood to try and find any stores with power, so we could try and charge our phones. When we arrived home, anything of value whether material or survival wise was gone. We had taken to surviving day by day ever since.

Maybe this is why we didn't leave when we heard the car. Maybe none of us had the energy to fight anymore. If they were looters, maybe murdering us and putting us out of our misery might be a relief.

The dusty, black jeep pulled up slowly beside our camp. I turned to my parents to see if they were going to react, but they just sat there slack jawed.

The window rolled down to reveal a well tanned man in thirties. He glanced at our sad fire for a second and then broke into a toothy grin.

"Well, how's it going there, folks?" He called out to us. He had the whitest teeth I had ever seen, and his canines were sharpened to points.

My father held up his hands and stammered, "We don't have very much sir, and we don't want any trouble. This is my wife Janice and my son Greg. I'm Ted Blinker and none of us want any harm,"

I could see the sweat forming on my father's forehead, and I clenched my fist, embarrassed at my father's weak display. My mother didn't even look up. She just kept her head down and determinedly stared at the ground.

"Well, you can put your hands down buddy," the stranger called leaning an arm out of his car, "I don't mean ya'll any harm. In fact, I'm here to offer you some help. You haven't had access to a radio lately have you."

My father shook his head and wiped fresh sweat from his brow.

"That's what I thought. Well my name is Benji and I'm part of a crew of folk who's trying to rebuild civilization. My job is to round up some kind folk like yourself and bring you back to camp, so you can be taken care of. We've got food, water, shelter, and a whole lot more than what you're working with here," Benji added with a nod towards our pitiful camp.

"How do we know your telling the truth?" My father asked. My mother didn't say a word. She just sat there watching the scene with interest. At least she finally looked up.

"Fair question," Benji replied and opened the door to his Jeep, "Well you are free to check the car and myself, you will find that there are no weapons on me. What you will find is food in the trunk and plenty of it. That could be your snack as we find our way back to campus."

My parents stared at each other for a moment and my mom gave a half hearted shrug. My father peered into the car nervously and motioned for me to pat Benji down.

Benji chuckled as I checked him. I found myself longing to punch him right in his grinning face.

"See, no weapons," He called to my father as we finished our inspection, "and if you look at the passenger's side seat you will see a small battery operated radio. Click the button on the right side. That will turn it on, and you'll be able to hear our little advertisement."

My father dragged a clumsy thumb across the button and soon the radio sprang to life.

"Attention all citizens! Attention! We at the Campus are here to help you! The Campus is a government run camp meant to help you during this trying time. We will provide you with food, water, shelter, and even power options at no cost to you! We are located at..."

Static flared up and made it impossible to hear the rest. My father smacked the radio a few times in his hand, but it seemed the radio had died.

"My batteries must have run out. Sorry folks, but you got the idea," Benji shoved his hands into his pockets and grinned all around, "Campus is only a few hours drive from here. You can sleep on the car ride and we'll be there just in time for breakfast!"

"What's the catch," I blurted out. I couldn't figure out why, but I didn't trust this man. Maybe it had something to do with that over the top smile.

"No catch. I swear," Benji responded by holding his hands out as a sign of peace, "We're just trying to help get people back on their feet. It doesn't cost anything. You may have to do a few chores here or there, we all have to pitch in a bit, but there's nothing to fret over."

"What sort of chores?" I pressed.

"Nothing crazy champ," Benji answered slapping me too hard on the arm, "Just things like helping to gather food or driving to collect folk like yourselves. Just enough so that your pitching in."

I saw my father glance back at my mother with excitement. He had popped open the trunk and was practically drooling over the cans of food. However, I was not convinced this was the saving grace Benji was trying to make this camp out to be.

"Again, what's the catch?" I asked, ignoring my father's annoyed glare, "This sounds a little too good to be true and there's still a lot of information you're leaving out."

"Please excuse my son," my father began, but was swiftly cut off as Benji took a casual step towards me and wrapped his arm around my shoulder.

"Smart questions kiddo." I winced at "kiddo" and briefly considered biting his hand so he would get off me.

"But I promise you," Benji continued, "There is no catch. This is just a volunteer organization to help people get back on their feet." He paused and pulled an old fashioned pocket watch out of his jeans pocket.

"Listen, I don't mean to pressure you guys, but if I don't start heading back soon, people are going to start to worry and I have no way of contacting anyone anymore. So I'll answer more questions as we make our way to the Campus, but you've got to make your minds on whether you're coming with me or not."

Instantly, my father nodded towards my mother. This was a chance for him to get out of the wild. More importantly, this was a chance for him to give up all responsibility to someone else. For my father this was an easy decision, the last thing he ever wanted to be was a leader.

My mother shrugged her shoulders and defeatedly started to make her way to her feet. At this point, Benji could have offered to shoot us in the head and I think she would have just accepted it. My mother's will died with the power.

I gritted my teeth and allowed Benji to guide me towards the jeep. It seemed the decision had been made without me.

We piled into the jeep. My father hauled himself into the passenger's seat while my mother and I huddled in the back with our few meager possessions. My father babbled his thanks. My mother silently peered out the window.

Even though I had many more questions, I decided to follow my mother's example. I gazed out the window. It was too dark to make much out. The power lines were long gone.

Fine. I thought to myself. If my parents want to go blindly with some stranger to who knows where then I wasn't going to argue any more. Maybe Benji is telling the truth and it really will be a refuge. We can finally go our separate ways and stop pretending we care about one another. Also, if Benji was leading us to some murder cult, then at least I could tell my parents I told you so.

DAY 95

My father's rambling soon started to falter. He glanced frequently at me to see if I was going to speak, but I continued to stare blankly out the window. No one wanted to hear my questions, so I wasn't going to say anything anymore. I was tired of putting myself out on a limb for strangers.

We drove in silence for a while. The hum of the car must have put me to sleep because, before I knew it, I was woken by the rumbling sensation of tires over stone. I glanced out the window. It was still fairly dark, early rays of the sunrise illuminated our surroundings.

We had definitely gone off the beaten path. In fact, we weren't even on the road anymore. We careened over a choppy path. Branches from the trees smacked against the window and dirt flew up from the tires.

I peeked at my father who was sound asleep and snoring lightly in front of me. Benji drove onward, but his expression was no longer the grinning salesman he had been earlier. He was clearly tired, and with the rising sun I could better see the lines and etches around his eyes and mouth. He stared forward without reaction to the jostling of the vehicle. On a closer glance, Benji was older than I first thought and a man on a mission.

My mother, on the other hand, seemed to have not moved an inch the entire drive. She just continued looking out her side of the window. I would comfortably bet she didn't sleep a wink the entire time.

I don't know what possessed me. But I had a sudden need to reach out to her, to make some sort of contact. I honestly couldn't remember the last time the last time I had been held by my mother.

Hesitantly, I stretched my arm out and grazed her arm. She jumped as if startled and twisted around to look at me. Blue meet blue, my mother and I had the same eyes. It was the one thing of hers that still had some beauty to them. She opened her mouth, but we must have hit a huge dip or hole in the ground, because we were suddenly lifted from our seats and thrown around the back seat of the car.

My mother and I yelped in unison, which must have woken my father who let out a short squeak of his own.

Benji threw his head back and laughed, "Whoa there folks! Hang on! It's going to be a bumpy ride!"

"Where are we?" My father asked bewildered.

"Mitchcreek Forest," Benji replied. His grinning mask had returned, "It's a state park, but it's small. People often forget about it, so it's been left fairly untouched from the rest of civilization. However, in the middle of the park there was a campground and a park ranger headquarters. It had food, supplies, first aid, basically what you need to survive in the wild. A few rangers brought their families during the very first few days of the power loss.

"We call it "The Incident" around here," may father interrupted.

"I would say that what happened was more than an incident. The chaos that happened when the power was lost was devastating. But those rangers were real heroes. Once they realized this area had some semblance of peace and survival they reached out to anyone they could for aid. They also started rescuing people and bringing them here. Soon, it grew to be the Campus we have today, and it's growing more and more everyday."

"Amazing," My father added, "Whatever happened to those original rangers?"

"Unfortunately, they died a while ago. A rescue mission gone awry. But we're established enough to continue everything in order, but of course they are constantly in our thoughts."

We drove in silence for a minute until a hoarse whisper came from beside me.

"How specifically did they die?"

I turned startled. I couldn't remember the last time I heard my mother's voice. It honestly took me a minute to even recognize it as hers.

"Jesus Janice, what a question!" My father called out in obvious shock.

"They were hung," Benji answered curtly. His smile had become a grimace, "A group of looters called 'The Tribe' wrangled them up and took them for everything they have. We never got to recover their bodies. They're still there, swinging from the trees, a warning now."

"Are they nearby?" My father quivered.

"They're a fair few miles off," Benji replied, "They won't come into our territory and if they do, we'll be ready." Benji trailed off until the car splashed into a shallow expanse of water roughly jostling all of us from side to side.

"Well on a brighter note," Benji chirped, "It seems that we've made good time! We'll be at the Campus in a moment!"

My mother and I exchanged a long look. Not a word was spoken, but, for once, we were connected, and we both knew our stay at the campus was not going to end well.

We passed through a series of small trees until we stopped in front of a wood cabin. It wasn't enormous, but it appeared practical and sturdy. There were no signs or decorations to be found from the outside.

Behind the cabin we saw the outlines of white tents fluttering in the morning breeze. People were hustling and bustling in and out of the cabin with purposeful expressions.

The car halted and Benji motioned for us to follow him. We made our way up the creaky steps and into the cabin.

The inside of the building was much more spacious than the outside suggested. There was a large main room with closed doors that lined the right and left sides. People buzzed in and out of those doors carrying various boxes and contraptions. We were led through a metal door into an office.

The office was bursting at the seams with random gadgets and gizmos. Shelves either side of the office stuffed with first aid kits and cans. There were dusty globes and binoculars of various sizes. Along one wide bookshelf, there were books that ranged in genre from nature books to children's picture stories. Facing the door was an enormous, oak desk with a black, leather chair behind it. Behind the desk, mismatched filing cabinets lined the wall. Above the filing cabinets was what appeared to be a large, black and white map of the forest and surrounding area.

Benji closed the door behind us, and I immediately began to feel claustrophobic. I couldn't stop thinking about all these shelves collapsing on me, leaving me crushed under junk and locked behind a steel door.

A sharp knock interrupted my thoughts and a tall man clomped into the office. He was dressed in tan khakis and his flannel shirt was torn at the sleeves. On his feet were large, steel toed hiking boots, and when he shook our hands, I noticed his hands were rough and scratched.

"Nice to meet you folks. My name is Randy."

Randy nodded at Benji and sat behind and propped his elbows onto the desk, "Sorry, I don't have any extra chairs to offer you. So how can I help you folks?"

"They want to join the Campus," Benji answered.

Randy eyed us and rubbed the scruff on his chin, "So they want to join us huh? Well I need to know two things; who are 'they' and why do they want to join us?"

"They are the Blinkers," Benji responded. Then he pointed to each of us, "That strapping fellow right there is Ted, the lovely lady next to him is his wife Janice, and this charming bugger on her other side is their son Greg. I found them trying to make camp a few miles off. At the rate they were going, there was no way they'd be able to survive the winter."

I clenched my jaw. I wanted to tell him that he didn't know what I was capable of. I wanted to scream at him for assuming that we were so weak.

"I have a good feeling about them Randy. They seem like good people and they're ready to work." Benji continued, slapping my father on the arm.

My father nodded enthusiastically, and I found myself torn on what I wanted to punch more; Benji's smug face or my father's pathetic doughy expression.

"What can they do?" Randy asked Benji, "What can they bring to the Campus?"

Nothing, unless you need someone to do your taxes or drink your wine, I thought. But my father spoke hurriedly for us, "My son is actually quite a good hunter and skinner and my wife can cook. I'll do whatever you need me to do."

I felt the heat rise in my face. My father's desperation was so embarrassing. Also, calling me a hunter and my mom a cook was the definition of an overstatement, but I kept my thoughts to myself.

Randy nodded slowly, but his gaze was still focused on Benji who just shrugged in return. Finally, Randy turned to us and sighed, "It's not all easy living here at the Campus. You get out of it what you put into it. But we support each other here. We all have each other's back. If you can't handle that, then you can't stay here."

"We can handle that," My father answered. I could see the longing in his eyes. He would do anything to not have to be in charge anymore.

Randy scanned my father's face for a second, and then clamped his hand down on the desk, "Well then, welcome aboard. Benji here will show you where you will be staying, and I'll have Brenda go over the rules with you and bring your supplies." Abruptly, Randy stood up and made his way around the desk and shook our hands a final time. His grip was strong, but I resisted to rub my hand. Randy told Benji to lead us to slot "R14," whatever that meant and then he made his way out the door without another word.

After a pause, Benji slapped my father on the back, "See I knew you folks would fit right in. I think you guys are really going to feel like family here soon." With that, Benji led us out of the office and to our new home.

* * *

We followed Benji to the back of the cabin. When we got there, we could see rows and rows of pure white tents. To the left and right there were thick, tall, pine trees that surrounded the camp like a dark green wall. Outside of these tents were people cooking, cleaning wash, and tending to children. No one bothered to look up as we passed, they were all too focused on the task at hand, and the ones who did see us, seem unfazed by newcomers.

It was a long walk before we arrived at our tent. We were the second to last tent in the row all the way over on the right side. Inside, the tent was bare but surprisingly large.

"You guys just make yourself cozy and I'll get your stuff from the car. Brenda will be over here soon to go over the details with you guys."

Benji left us and we laid down in our empty tent, "I think this is really going to work out guys," my father announced. My mother and I didn't even nod, we just turned our backs to him and laid down.

Light shone through the cloth of the tent and I found myself longing for my phone. I missed the comfort of holding it in my hand. It was always something I could turn to when I was sad, or bored -- my little metal teddy bear.

The entrance of the tent flapped open, and I rolled over to see a middle aged woman holding a large cardboard box. Her face was heavily lined and there was a severe sag in her chin, but her eyes were a sharp bright blue.

"You the Blinkers?" She asked matter-of-factly.

We nodded and she placed the box carefully on the ground, "I'm Brenda. I've been living here for a fair while and I'll help get you set up with everything."

We stared as she pulled a first aid kit out of the box, followed by a filled canteen, multiple cans of food, and a heat lamp, "We'll bring you sleeping bags and the rest of your supplies in a little bit. I've only got two hands. But I want to go over the rules in a bit more detail with you guys and also let you know how the next couple of days are going to work."

She sat crossed legged on the ground and pulled a piece of paper out of her jean jacket. "So the rules of the campus are pretty straight forward. Keep your area clean. You will be given a ration of food and water weekly, make sure to use it wisely."

We gaped at the food. It had been ages since we have seen so much of it, and the fact that it was just handed freely out to us was overwhelming. I was very curious to find out how they had come to so much food, but I decided it was in my best interest not to ask.

Brenda ignored our shock and carried on with her speech, "You'll have the first two days to look around the camp and get yourselves settled. On the third day you will be assigned a job. Everyone here has to contribute in some way, and if you don't pull your weight you'll be forced to leave."

The tent parted, and Brenda nodded as two men entered and dropped off sleeping bags and another cardboard box. Then she continued her speech.

"The rest of the rules are pretty straight forward. No fighting, no stealing, do what your told, keep your head down and keep your noses clean. If you do that then you should have no problems here. If you can't then I don't recommend making yourself comfortable."

With that, Brenda hoisted herself back onto her feet, "If you have any questions, my tent is A12. It's right in front of the campus, almost directly behind the office. You can stop by and ask me. If I'm not available, then you can always go into the office and find someone there to help you out. Some more people will be stopping by to help you out over the next few days as well. So for now, why don't you eat and get yourselves some rest."

Brenda turned to leave, but as she stepped one foot out of the tent, she stopped and spun around, "One last thing," Brenda announced. "This is important, so listen up. You need to understand we may be a friendly community, but there are other folks around here who aren't so charitable. They're mangy, but cunning and they want what we have. You are not and I mean not," With this Brenda stepped forward to emphasize her point, "Not to ever speak to these people. They will do anything they can to infiltrate the community, and if they do, it will be the end of everything we have built here. That means the end of safety for you."

"Understood," My father responded, but Brenda shook her head.

"You need to swear it. I can not say this any more plainly. If you are found working with one of these rival groups. You will be thrown out of the Campus immediately, and that's if you're lucky. So swear it on everything you love."

"I swear on my family," My father announced, and my mother shook her head, but the concern in her eyes was plain.

"I swear on my family too," I said. This seemed to please Brenda who nodded and made our way out of the tent.

My father gave my shoulder a weak squeeze and moved to examine the cans Brenda had brought to us. I laid back on my side and closed my eyes, giving my word to Brenda had been easy. It was easy to swear on something that you didn't love.

DAY 98

The next two days passed by quickly. I explored the Campus. No one really paid much mind to me or my parents, who blended in immediately. I soon learned the Campus was not as big as it first made itself out to be. The cabin which was the source of supplies and order, along with the rows of tents were imposing, but otherwise the campus was made up of a few outhouses, man made wells, and fire stations.

A few armed men patrolled the border between the campus and the woods that surrounded us. I learned quickly we were not allowed into these woods unless we were assigned to be, and for that, we needed official paperwork.

I was actually relieved on the third day to be assigned a job. The Campus was starting to feel dull, and there was nothing I despise more than being bored.

When we still had power, I always had something to keep me entertained -- games at the palm of my hand, videos from people all over the world, instant contact to my friends. Now there was nothing to distract, nothing to numb the world.

I was even more excited to find out I was going to be a hunter for the campus. My parents and I were called upon early on the third morning. Before us stood Brenda, and two burly men.

When the jobs were announced, I saw my parents looks of concern, but I ignored them completely. I was starting to feel claustrophobic being trapped in this little world and I wanted to see what was around us. So, without even bothering to stay and hear what my parents were assigned, I grabbed the paperwork needed to enter the forest, and left for my work.

I followed one of the men to the outskirts of the forest. He introduced himself as Charlie. Charlie had a thick, red beard, streaked with gray and hands like baseball mitts. At the entrance to the forest were two other people, a middle aged woman named Ramona whose husky voice suggested she used to smoke at least a pack a day before "The Incident." The other hunter was an older teenager named Art.

Art was exceptionally tall, but lean and with such a terrible case of acne, it looked painful. We made our quick introductions and then Charlie handed me a knife and crossbow.

"Bullets are a precious commodity around here," Charlie explained. "We only use them when absolutely necessary, which means we're not wasting them on some critter."

I was tempted to ask what was important enough to bring out the guns but bit my tongue. At this point, it was probably better not to know.

"So to catch us some meat, we have to go about it the old fashioned way with arrows and traps. The weather has been getting colder lately, so that means the animals have been scarcer. Today we're branching out into some new territory to see if we can get enough to tide the Campus over for a bit. So we can't be fooling around out there. We need to work quickly, quietly, and cleanly. Do you understand?"

I nodded, but my heart pounded. Sure I had snagged a few squirrels here or there while we were on the road, but I certainly was no professional. I looked into the dark tangle of the forest and back to the white fluttering tents of the campus. What if I didn't catch anything? What if I made a fool out of myself? I knew there was no way I would be able to survive on my own if I was thrown out of the campus. My mother and father were probably sitting pretty with some cushy, safe job, and now because my father had to open his stupid mouth, I had to throw myself to the wolves.

"Since this is a new path, make sure to keep your eyes open for people as much as animals," Art stated as his grip tightened around his knife.

"Good point, Art," Charlie added, "People are more dangerous than the critters around these parts. So if you see anyone, make sure to let us know right away."

I nodded again, but I could feel the beads of sweat start to form at my temple.

"Randy told us your father said you could hunt," Ramona wheezed, looking me up and down. "Let's see if he was telling the truth."

I sniffed and followed the trio into the forest. I had to prove myself a hunter. I was going to kill something in these woods if it was the last thing I did.

* * *

Charlie led the way through the woods with Ramona behind him. No one spoke. I glanced at Art, who was walking beside me. For such an uncoordinated looking kid he walked with surprising stealth. His eyes darted back and forth, and his hand never left his knife.

I wondered what had happened to him -- who his parents were. He wasn't that much older than me, maybe before all of this we could have been friends. That is, if I actually knew how to make human friends.

There was a clear path at the beginning of the hike, but after a time, the forest floor became more dirt and gnarled roots. Thankfully though, winter was fast approaching so many of the trees had lost their leaves allowing glimmers of sunshine to help guide the way.

I had never been camping before "The Incident," but I had heard from adults about appreciating the beauty of nature. Right now, in the quiet morning with the frost tinted trees, I suppose I could have found the entire scene serene, but I didn't. I was tired. I was cold and I missed my old life. Why bother with the discomfort of the outside world when you could pull up visions of the most spectacular places on earth, while curled up in your favorite pajamas. The more time I spent without power, the more I realize how much the real world just plain sucks.

Suddenly, Art halted and let out a sharp hiss. I turned and saw him bend down. I followed his gaze to an injured buck laying hidden amid a tangle of bushes. Art had sharp eyes, the buck was fairly well hidden, though his size and horns gave him away.

Charlie pulled out his crossbow and I wrapped my hand around mine as well. This bugger could provide us with a good amount of meat. It'd be a triumphant start to my hunting career.

Charlie held up one hand. We waited breathlessly for his signal. Then he swept down his hand and I fired my arrow.

I missed completely. It flew to the right and impaled itself into a tree. Charlie's arrow, however, flew straight and true and struck the deer directly in the side of the neck.

I watched in horror as it laid bleeding and wild eyed. But, in a flash Art and Ramona jumped up and ended the poor animals suffering.

Charlie patted my arm, "You'll get it next time," He reassured me. Then he went bounding with excitement over to the corpse. The three of them were chattering with excitement, but all I could think of was the pain in the buck's eyes as the blood pooled around him.

I turned and vomited loudly on the ground, gripping a tree for stability. I was pathetic. Weak. I should never have survived this long. Humiliated, I looked up with tear stained eyes to see Ramona and Charlie laying with their throats slit on the ground.

Art was standing with his arms in the air as a lumbering man pointed a shotgun at him. He was flanked on either side by adults in military camouflage armed to the teeth.

I thought about running away, warning the people of the Campus, or just scurrying in the woods to try and make it on my own. But my feet wouldn't obey. So instead, I sunk to my knees and raised my hands to the air. This would have been the time to pray for help or forgiveness, but I didn't know how.

A stocky, bald man crept forward and pointed a revolver at my head, "You lot from Campus?" He asked.

"Yes." I immediately blurted out. Art remained silent.

A couple people grumbled and spat on the ground, but the bald man kept his gaze and his gun pointed at me.

"You want to know who I am, boy. My name is Eric. I was one of the rangers that first built that little community. I tried following their rules, but it was all bullshit. Why should I get the same amount of food as the slugs who sat around mashing leaves? Why should I have to share my valuable supplies with strangers who I didn't even know I could trust. I wasn't being selfish. I was being smart."

There was a grumble of agreements from his companions. I didn't know why he was telling me this, but I felt it would be better not to ask.

But Eric ignored his companions and continued, "We were constantly taken adventage of. We brought people in and they would steal our goods and make off into the night, or try and slit us in our throats as we slept. I didn't want to bring in anymore people. I wanted to build on the people we had. Make them stronger, smarter, a perfect society in this new world. My friends turned me away, forced me and my fellow rangers out into the wild to die. Dear old Randy lied and told the rest of the community that some rebel group called 'The Tribe' killed us. But I didn't die now did I son."

I shook my head, my arms were shaking from the strain, but I refused to put them down.

"No. I thrived," Eric continued, "We made a new community of our own. A stronger world, with benefits you could only dream of, and I got my revenge on those cocksucking rangers who betrayed me.”

I remembered Benji's story about the past rangers and my stomach turned. Eric was now so close to me that I could feel the cold steel of the barrel against my forehead.

“But I'm not done with the Campus. Not even close. You two are young, so unlike the others I'm going to give you a choice; you can either choose to not help me and end up with your brains splattered like your puke against this tree, or you can help me destroy the Campus. You can come back with us and all be set with more food and supplies than you'll ever need. Also...”

Eric bent onto one knee and pulled something out of his pocket that I thought I would never see again, a phone, and it was working.

“How did you...” But Eric cut me off.

“We've got power. Real power. I can tell you all about how I came to get this later, But now, you have to make a choice. You can either help me and live with power or end up like your buddies on the ground.”

It can't be. It's not possible. But there it was glowing back at me, like an old friend waiting with open arms. I could relax and not have to try so hard. I could be taken care of again, instead of being the one to do all of the caring.

The words were out of my mouth before I could even give them a second thought,

“Deal.”

At the same time I heard Art yell, “Fuck off,” and before I knew it his head was cleanly sliced off his neck and his zitty face was rolling towards me.

“Good choice,” Eric replied, nodding towards Art's head. He reached out his hand to me and I took it. He pulled me to my shaky feet.

“What's your name son?” Eric asked.

“Greg,” I whispered as tears and snot mixed together on my face.

“Well let's get you cleaned up and get this party started.” Eric then gave a signal to his crew and they began to creep back into the forest. I stared down at the bodies of my Campus members. My head was buzzing, but through the static one question came more clearly then all the rest.

"Eric, could I please hold the phone?"

* * *

I followed Eric's group for what must have been miles. He didn't let me hold the phone, but I could see it glowing through his pocket like a beacon. We finally broke through the edge of a forest and I saw something bright shining ahead of me. No way, could it be lights? Real electrical lights?

I quickened my pace, but Eric pulled me by the scruff of the neck and tossed me onto the ground.

"Don't get too excited now chief. Before we let you into our little sacred haven, you're going to have to hold up your end of the deal. Tell us about the Campus. Every little detail you can think of. Also," Eric grabbed me by the front of my shirt and pulled me so close to his face that the spit from his mouth splattered onto my nose. "If we find out you're lying or keeping something from us, you're not going to get as quick of an ending as your buddies back there in the woods."

I told. I told them everything I knew -- where everything was located, how many tents I could remember, what supplies were available to us, the names of everyone I could think of, including my parents.

Eric sat cross-legged on the dirt and calmly listened to every word I said. His face was like an untouched pool. Relaxed, serene even, he didn't even react until I mentioned my mother and father.

"You know when we go through with this, it's not going to end well for them, your parents I mean," Eric stated matter-of-factly. "Are you willing to live with that?"

Could I? This question should have been difficult. I should be worried about the fate of my parents. I should feel guilty for betraying them. I should want to protect them. I should feel anything.

But I didn't have any of those feelings. I felt nothing. So I looked Eric dead in the eye and said, "I can deal with that."

He held my stare for a while, some strange, unspoken staring contest. Finally, he tore his eyes away from me and snapped to a man behind him. The man handed Eric a gun, and Eric handed the gun to me. The silver glinted in the unnatural light as I held it between my hands.

DAY 99

Eric left to speak with his other companions about the plan to sack the campus. Before Eric left, I was tied to a tree "just to be safe." But before Eric left, he tossed his phone to the ground. It was so close that I could almost drag it to me with my foot, but yet it was still so far away.

I writhed in the ropes. They weren't tied very tightly, so I was able to inch my leg closer and closer to the phone. It must have been hours later, but when my toe grazed the device, I felt my heart start to pound with excitement. I needed this. It had been so long since I held any sort of electronic in my hand. Using my foot, I slide the phone closer and closer. My fingertips were just about to graze the phone when a heavy, black boot kicked the phone away.

"Not yet. We've got work to do."

When I looked up at Eric, I saw nothing but red. I felt nothing, but pure, adult rage, and I wanted nothing more than to bury my nails into his face and claw his eyes out.

"I told you everything I know, and all you've done is boss me around and tie me up. What more do you need from me now!" I whined. I kicked and writhed with tears coming unbidden down my cheeks. It was childish to throw a tantrum, but I didn't even care. I just wanted to feel normal again and Eric kicked that moment away from me.

Eric bent down and picked up the phone, sliding it into his pocket before turning back to me. "I know you've been through a lot so far buddy, and you've definitely talked the talk. But now it's time for you to walk the walk. Come help us destroy the Campus, and I'll give you one of these bad boys all for yourself. You'll be living large. I promise."

I could see the glow of the phone through his pocket, and my heart ached for it. I sniffled and nodded as Eric's crew untied me.

"I may not trust you with a phone yet," Eric handed me an object wrapped in brown cloth, "But I am trusting you with this."

I removed the cloth and held a round of bullets in my hand.

"You know how to shoot?" Eric asked loading the gun he gave me.

"Kind of," I replied. I had never shot a gun before in real life, but I shot them countless times in my games. How much different could it really be?

"You point at your target and click the trigger. That's about it. This baby's tiny, so you don't need to worry about a lot of kickback. Safety's off though, so try, try not to shoot yourself in the leg."

Eric slapped me on the back and motioned to someone behind him. A team of people emerged behind him, all seemingly armed. No one spoke and no one smiled. Everyone just looked forward with the same expression of grim determination.

"You ever shoot a person?" Eric whispered in my ear. He looked at my face, reading my expression. I didn't answer. Of course I had never shot a person, but I didn't want Eric to know that. I didn't want these people thinking I was any weaker than they already did.

"Well, if you haven't" Eric murmured, "today's going to be a first for you."

Eric waved to his people, and they quietly began moving forward into the dark. I looked down at the gun in my hands. Could I do it? Could I actually kill a real person? It was one thing to shoot fake terrorists and enemies online, but could I actually look someone in the eye and take their life?

I couldn't answer my own questions. The honest truth was that I didn't really know. All I knew was that I could still faintly see the outline of the phone through Eric's pocket and I knew wherever that phone went, that's where I had to be. So I carefully, put the gun through the loop of my pants and followed him.

We marched in a single file until we reached the spot in the forest where Eric first found me.

"Circle up," Eric uttered and three groups split up in separate directions. I had no idea where I was supposed to go, so I stayed with Eric in the last remaining group.

"Torches," Eric commanded, and a group member handed each of us a wooden torch wrapped in cloth and a lighter.

"When I give the signal," Eric commanded in hushed tones, "Light the torches. Burn the tents but try to leave the cabin. That's where most of the supplies are and we don't want to lose that. Gather what tools you can, destroy the rest, and I do mean the rest. Leave no survivors." He gave each of us a meaningful look. He locked his eyes onto mine, but I just looked down, clenching my fists tightly to keep them from shaking.

"Let's go," Eric ordered.

We made our way through a small trail in the forest. I saw the tips of the tents like small, white sails in my line of view. Eric motioned for us to line up around him. We were soon connected to members of the three other groups. Together, we formed one giant circle around the Campus. Once everyone was in position, Eric waved his arm forward, and we inched our way forward silently.

When we just feet away from the Campus. Eric held his hand up to stop us. He then held up his lighter and lit his torch. Around me, others ignited their torches as well. Hesitantly, I flicked open my lighter, and after a few clumsy attempts, started the flame.

It must have been late. The Campus was so quiet the only noise that could be heard was the crackling of fire. I tried to hold my fire aloft like the others, but soon my arm started to ache and tremble and I had to grasp it with two hands.

Who am I kidding? I can't do this? I can barely hold this damn light, and lord knows what will happen if I actually need to use my other hand to reach and grab my gun. I'm pathetic. There's no way I should have lived this long. I've made a terrible mistake.

Eric held up his index finger, everyone leaned towards the Campus, steadying themselves for the attack. Sweat pooled under my arms and along my forehead. Maybe when they go forward, I can just linger in the back. They won't even notice I'm not there. Maybe I should just shit my pants and run into the woods to die like the coward I am.

Eric pointed forward and nodded to the left and to the right. It was time. Groups stealthily broke from the circle and charged forward with their torches held high, until my group was the only one left.

Finally, Eric lunged ahead and unleashed a primal scream. Without thinking, I followed him into the thick of the chaos. The yells of Eric's people joined his and became one wild battle cry.

I just ran. I ran past burning tents and screaming families. The smoke burned my eyes and filled my throat making me choke. Frustrated, I threw the torch onto the ground and coughed and spat onto the ground. I looked up to see ash falling around me like black snow. I watched a woman sprinting through the Campus with boxes of supplies tucked under her arms. Shots ran loudly around me, and I saw a Benji get his throat slit by a teenage girl who didn't even blink an eye.

Randy rushed out with a shotgun, but he was plowed down by Eric, who just fired bullet after bullet, even when it was clear that Randy was very dead. Eric wasn't shooting in defense. He was shooting out of rage.

All around me, there was death, fire, and blood. I scrambled to my feet. I had to think of something. I had to do something. But my brain wouldn't work. So I did what came instinctively to me. I ran.

***

I ran past bodies, and looting. I tried to keep count in my head of the rows and numbers of tents. I finally recognized the tent my parents and I were assigned too, and I dived inside of it.

There was no one inside. I didn't know what to do. So I curled up in the corner of the tent and pulled my knees to my chest as my breath started to hitch. I couldn't do this. I couldn't do any of this. Maybe I could just hide out here and hope that no one notices me. Perhaps they'll forget me, and I'll be able to slip away, or maybe someone will just light this god damn tent on fire and finish me off already.

Suddenly, the flaps of the tent were pulled back and my parents stumbled through.

"Greg," my father cried, "Oh, Thank God! We were so worried about you!"

My mother didn't say anything. But I saw her tense face sag with relief. I should have been glad to see them. I should have rushed into their arms and cried or tried to make a plan to get out of here. I should have felt something, but instead I felt numb and clung onto my knees more tightly.

"We've gotta get out of here," My father yelled glancing fervently over his shoulder, "Grab what you can and then let's make a run for it!"

My mother and father hurried around the tent gathering what cans and goods they could. When they were finished, they turned to look at me.

"Come on Greg, We've got to make a move on!" My father insisted his eyes darting frantically.

I didn't move. I couldn't. My mind couldn't process what was happening and my body seemed to have taken on a mind of its own. All I could do was keep my eyes trained to the corner of the tent in front of me.

"Greg! I am ordering you to get up right now!" My father screamed. It was the first time I ever heard my father raise his voice. I suppose I should have found this intimidating, but I could hear the crack of fear in his voice when he yelled. Instead of fear, all I felt was pity. I felt pity for this poor, little mouse trying to imitate a man. So, still I didn't move.

"Greg!" My father bellowed. I could see the panic written all over his face. I wondered when he would finally succumb to his cowardice and just make a run for it and leave me behind.

I heard a sharp intake of breath from my mother, and I finally turned away from the corner and saw what had given her a start.

Eric was standing in the entrance of the tent. One hand rested in his pocket while another held his gun which was cocked towards my mother's head.

"Evening," Eric greeted my parents then he turned to me, "Greg I'm so glad I found you. I was wondering where you went. But, you're here and you've even managed to track down some of the last survivors. Why don't you finish this up, so we can mosey our way out of here."

I turned my head back and forth between Eric and my parents gaping faces.

"What do you mean, finish this up?" I stuttered and Eric rolled his eyes.

"I told you at the very beginning of this raid that we couldn't leave any survivors." Eric responded and then nodded at my parents, "It's nothing personal. It's just if we leave anyone alive, old angers can brew and everything just gets mighty messy."

I froze and my parents looked on in horror.

"No. Please," my father begged, "We'll leave right now. You'll never hear from us again. I swear."

"You see, I'd love to believe you," Eric sighed, "But we just can't take chances. Not in the world we live in now."

Eric then turned so that his gun was now directly pointed at me, "Well son, let's go. Get it done quick. No point in making these poor people suffer."

"But…" I started, but my father interrupted.

"He's our son!"

"Is he now," Eric exclaimed and narrowed his eyes at my parents and I, "Now that you say it, I do see the resemblance. You definitely take after your momma Greg. But, if I do recall Greg, we had a conversation about this very situation, and you made me a promise. You don't want to be a liar now do you."

"I can't do it…" I cried.

"Take out your gun," Eric barked.

I grabbed the gun from my side. My hands were shaking so hard I dropped the gun to the ground and had to scramble to pick it up.

"Alright son, now I had a feeling you were new to this, so I'm going to walk you through this step by step. First, aim your gun towards one of your parents," Eric said this all calmly, as if he were trying to teach a kid how to ride a bike.

"Please, I…" I wept.

"Greg. Aim it towards one of your parents. I'm letting you choose who dies first, but if you need, I can decide that too. If you don't. I'm just going to shoot the three of you and I really don't want to do that to you Greg."

Trembling, I raised the gun and pointed it between my parents. I shouldn't do this. I should just let Eric kill us all and be done with it, But, a little voice whispered in the back of my mind. Who are these people to me? Yes, they might be my family by name, but when have they ever actually acted like a real mom and dad. They didn't teach me. They didn't spend time with me unless they had to. We didn't even like each other, and I certainly couldn't remember a time where we actually said I love you to one another.

Why should I risk my life for this facade? We were miserable together. Why not just end it and give them some peace and myself a chance to finally have what I want?

"Greg. Please." My father pleaded.

I chose. I shot. Blood splattered out of my father's chest as he crumpled to the ground. He laid wide eyed and slack jawed on the ground. His babbling had finally ceased.

"Nicely done Greg," Eric stated, inching his foot away from the growing puddle of blood so his boot wouldn't get dirty, "Now you can't just leave your momma all alone now. No need to drag it out for her. End it and then let's go."

I looked into my mother's eyes and saw my own. My finger froze on the trigger.

"Hmmm," Eric interjected after assessing the situation, "I've got to admit that I can see how this would be difficult for you there Greg. But you know what, I've been pretty harsh with you, and you can't expect something out of people for nothing. So here's the deal,"

Eric then pulled something out of his pocket. A phone, but it was different from the one I saw before. It was almost new, and the home screen called to me like a siren.

"Do this and you'll be made in the shade Greg. Again, I promise you and I'm a man of my word, unlike the folks around here," Eric added waving his gun, "You'll have all the technology we possess, and we'll set you up nice and comfy. After what we got today, you won't have to scavenge, hunt, or even really work for a long time. You can just curl up with the cell here and connect."

Connect. I wouldn't have to think. I wouldn't have to work. I can be part of the online world, my real world again. It could be like it was before. I turned to my mother and saw a single, silent tear roll down her cheek.

It was a difficult decision. But I knew what I had to do. In the end, I had to choose my family.

I shot. Blood bloomed from my mother's chest like a flower. One tear followed another as she crumpled to the ground.

I stared at her form. I had expected to have some reaction, crying, yelling, or guilt. But, in the end I just felt tired. I wanted to lay down. I didn't want to be present anymore.

"Well done Greg," Eric muttered, "I know that must have been hard."

I didn't even look at him. I just held my hand out expectantly. My hand tingled as the cold metal hit my palm. My fingers wrapped around the phone and a familiar feeling filled my chest. Home.

"You ready to go now son?" Eric asked.

I nodded and followed him back into the forest and the dark unknown. I'll never know if the real bad guy was Eric or the Campus. I'll never know if I did the right thing. I don't know how I'll live knowing I killed my mother and father moving forward.

But what I did know was that I finally had a family again.

WHAT THE MOON SAYS

BY MAX MCCAMISH

DAY 18

When a tree falls in a forest, nobody is around to hear it, but it still makes a sound. When every tree in the forest begins to fall at once, nothing changes for that first fallen tree at all.

The clouds of light in the sky behind the stars are new, as is the silent eeriness that coats much of the city and many faces when the sun has left. Not much else has changed from three weeks before. I shuffle the same through the streets, and the cold that lingers in the air and my fingertips is as present as always, always. People's distrust of me feels like the same heavy weight inside, beneath and behind my sternum, although it is directed from faces that had once known something a little warmer than these asphalt and concrete beds. Some are kinder and some less so, but all in all there are more huddled in the shadows than there had been before. Not everyone; many homes lit themselves with fires and continued on. Same as always, always.

I swipe at a bug on the back of my hand and sigh. Abandoned cars are a good place to look for things useful for Lexi and me, and that's a help, but I would be coming back with nothing except a wire that no longer conducts anything. It's wrapped around my fingers, trailing along the ground. I walk slow to keep the heat in and keep attention out, but she still catches my eye anyway.

She stands on the concrete between lanes of the road, sheltering under the bridge. I know on sight she is to be trusted, as I always know. Her hair is long and black and twisted around itself, her eyes shine and her demeanour is kindred with the world she walks in. She looks up at the moon and waits for it to speak to her, but it doesn't just speak to anyone. I do, however.

"Are…" my voice stutters, falling from my lips before the words are ready… "are you alright?"

She cocks her head like she struggles to understand me. Many did, so I paid it nothing. "I…" She's crying, and it breaks her words into little pieces like mine… "I don't think so. I don't know wh-where I am or how to g-get home."

"Home? Where's home?" She could be anywhere between fourteen and twenty-five. "I could know."

"I just need to get to Canada. If -- if I could get to the border I'm sure I could get home, I just -- I have no way of contacting anyone, but…"

She shakes, it might be the cold or it might not be. Her clothes are not meant for winter or the dark, colourful and bright such that she couldn't hide from anyone, her legs bare except for socks the color of pink highlighter. "I don't know how to get there."

I have no other response except, "I could take you to the border." I had no ties except Lexi and no reason to stay in the city's heart. "If you will come with me."

She looks up with doe eyes at me. "You know how to get there?" she says as though it's hard. "How can I repay you?"

I nod at her as I follow the path back to Lexi, and then shake my head to her second question. "Follow me. Your name is?"

She almost jumps to follow me, and when she stands beside me on the pavement, she's so much smaller than she seemed. "Clara," she answers easily. She has earrings that jangle as she takes every step. "And you are?"

She sounds excited to listen to me, a rare thing that warms that feeling inside, beneath and behind my sternum. "Maddox," I say, "that is what my friends call me."

"Is that your first name?" Clara asks, falling in step; I quicken my stride and she doesn't struggle to keep pace. "It's a funny one."

"It's not," I tell her, and the air between us feels clear, communication easy in a way it, with many, is not. My words twist and sound funny to strange ears far too often. Lexi says she needs a dictionary to interpret me. "But nobody calls me John."

"Can I?" she says, and it makes me laugh but I don't know why. I don't laugh often.

"If you want to," I say, taking a sharp turn to find Lexi. There's a back alley like a crack in the road above, and it's where we've been hiding for a few days now. In the pitch black, illuminated by nothing but a moon that won't talk to me and help me right now, it's best found by rote memorisation and that is what I do. Normally there are factories here, but the once ever-crunching, omnipresent noises and machinations stopped when the world did. Time moves on but it hardly feels like the present day anymore.

Clara hesitates. "Is this the way to the border?"

"No," I admit to her, "but we have to find my friend and my stuff before we go anywhere. I can't leave her, or it."

"Who's your friend?" Clara asks, that answer satiating her and making her safe. "Would I know her? I know many people."

"I don't think so," I admit, something itching under my skin. "She's kind."

Lexi is kind, and that was what I knew upon seeing her that turned out to be true. When the things I know are not always true, it is difficult to trust, but she has been around when nobody else has been and held onto me when nobody else would or could or should. How long I've known her is a question I struggle to answer; my memory doesn't stretch as far back as it perhaps should.

When I turn into the crack, Lexi is laying on my backpack, her hands tucked under her coat and her hair covering her face. She's asleep, and although I would have liked to bring back food for more than the day's that we have, the only thing I bring is instead someone to help. "Lexi, wake up."

"Where is she?" Clara asks, and I turn to her, that clear air feeling tainted now. I gesture and she looks past Lexi. "I don't see anyone, John."

I turn to Lexi, who shuffles in place. Her hair, too, is long and black, but it's a tangled straight, and she pushes it out of the way easily. "How'd it go, Maddox? Anything interesting?"

"I found this," I say, offering up the cord, "and I found Clara."

"You found…?" Lexi says, clarifying my words.

Clara turns to me and demands to know, "who are you talking to? Are you okay, John? Should I leave?"

"No, don't leave." Lexi frowns at me as I turn to Clara, reaching out to touch her shoulder; she dodges away from me like I might burn her. "Lexi, this is Clara, and I told her I'd take her to the border because that's how she's going to get home, okay?"

Clara bites her tongue, looking in the direction where Lexi is without her eyes landing on her. "Uh- please do take me to the border. Now, maybe? I know it's dark, but… I don't…"

Lexi takes a long time to answer. "You want to go to the border, Maddox?"

"Canadian border." I tilt my head. "To take Clara home."

"Yes, uh, that's what I want," Clara says, looking nervously around. She does not stand close to me.

Lexi sighs and shakily gets to her feet. She has a large frame that is not as suited to strength and endurance as mine is, and her eyes are a ghostly blue that I found hard to trust when I met her first; I trusted everything but her eyes. But the moon was reflected in them, and I trusted the moon and that lead me to trusting her and that was right. "I don't see why we can't go. We might find more luck leaving the city, anyway. God knows how it's going to be anywhere but here, but if you want to go…"

"Are we going?" Clara asks, jumping up and down a little bit on her feet.

"Now?" I clarify, turning to Lexi. Her face shows nothing about how she feels, and it probably wouldn't even if I could read her. She looks me up and down and the wire I hold in my hand and decides.

"You want to go now?" She sounds like she hardly believes me, but she's far too worn to mention much more than that. "It's dark, Maddox. I just woke up."

Pushing her out of her comfort is not what I want to do. I look at Clara. "It's dark."

Clara crosses her arms. "It's always dark. It's probably only like, nine. If you don't want to take me just point me in the right direction and I'll figure it out from there."

I want her to make sense. "Lexi doesn't want to go right now, and I don't want to leave her behind."

"I… look, I don't want to be rude or anything, but what the fuck are you talking about? Are you off your meds? Who the fuck is Lexi?" She extends her hands around in a circle, saying, "you and I are alone in an alleyway. Please just help me get to the border."

I turn to Lexi one last time. "I'm sorry. Clara wants to go to the border, and I promised her, I promised her…" Asking, not telling. I won't leave without her.

Lexi sighs a deep sigh, stretching her hands out above her head. She has walked these streets for a long time and is bothered by little. "Okay." There is a smile that knows something, one that is kind, but sadness lingers beneath. "We can go to the border now. We've just got to make sure you sleep sometime soon, alright?"

I nod, and she rises to her feet. I take my bag and put it across my shoulders; I loop the wire around its strap, and the heavy flashlight put in its side pocket. I release and inspect. The battery is long dead and batteries have been gold for almost three weeks now, but it is made of metal and heavy, taken from someone who took it from police. I press the button and it does not flicker, and I put it away, wondering if I'll ever see it flicker again. Clara looks apprehensive.

"Are we going?" she asks, at much the same time as Lexi suggests I grab my torch.

I say yes to both and take the piece of wood and the lighter from where they are inside my bag. There is cloth around the wood I set aflame, and a light guides us -- a light not taken even when all other light is gone. Except the sun and the moon, who remain silent above us, looking down on the earth so suddenly dark and quiet underneath them.

"That's smart," Clara says. Her hands are deep in the pockets of her shorts, and she doesn't seem as cold as she should be; she looks at the fire almost untrustworthily. "You must've been fine all this time."

"Everyone but us hasn't been fine," I tell her, "but little changes for us."

Lexi pays me no attention, looking instead at the way the firelight dances off the bricks beside us. It dances on her face, too, lighting a sun underneath her skin that I feel I am the only one to know.

"How long have you been out here?" Clara asks as we step out. "And can I ask why?"

"A while," I respond as the real answer evades my memory. There's something correct but I can't recall it. "Lexi, how long have we been out here?"

"I mean, I've been homeless for almost a year now. I think you've been homeless for much longer, but I don't know, why?"

I turn to Clara. "Yeah."

Clara frowns, and it needles at me. "You didn't answer my question."

"Oh." I crane my neck; communication is hard, and it's an outside pull I like to draw away from, shrink from like Clara does from the firelight, from me. She'll talk, but she won't come too close, not since being introduced to Lexi. "I don't know about me, but Lexi's been homeless for almost a year now."

"Okay, dude, John, Maddox, whatever. Please stop talking to people who don't exist. It's freaking me out a little bit, okay?"

"You're being rude to Lexi and I don't appreciate that. I don't," I say, walking a little bit faster. Lexi struggles to keep up with me while Clara does so easily, skipping along beside me.

"What…" Lexi begins, looking at me sidelong. "You're not talking to me, are you?"

"No I am not," I let her know, "you are fine. Clara is being rude to you."

"You're not going to stop doing it, are you?" Clara asks, arms crossed. "At least tell me what this ghost says."

I choose to ignore her, moving on ahead, as the firelight penetrates a darkness that has clothed the city ash-like for weeks now. Fire is all that breaks it up. For the first night, people came out with their candles and talked like the power would come back on any moment, until it didn't. Phones died and internet was down and that's when the freaking out began. In the darkness I watched it all and saw them all fall further down than they'd ever been and wondered how it happened.

"What caused the blackout?" Clara asks after the silence lasted a few minutes. "Do you know?"

"I don't," I tell her. "Lexi, you don't know, do you?"

"Don't know what?" She crosses her arms, the chill of winter getting to her even under a few layers of clothes.

"What caused the blackout."

"We've talked about this, Maddox." Her words are angry, but her tone is not, and I believe the latter. "I have no more idea than you or anyone else does."

I look to Clara. "Lexi doesn't know either."

"Thanks for at least relaying," Clara says begrudgingly. "I was hoping someone would know, but nobody does. I've been lost for weeks and I have no idea if my family is even alive."

"Who's your family?"

Lexi goes to answer before realising I'm not talking to her. She turns aside, the firelight catching on her tangled hair and reflecting it, almost like it's catching alight itself. I scratch at a bug on my hand.

"My mum's in the parliament in Canada," Clara says, "that's why I can find her if I just get across the border. But my phone's dead and I can't call, and I can't even find a car or anything because car batteries are dying so everyone's super protective of it. And I guess I don't have a job anymore if there's no internet."

"Alright." Her reaction politely whispers that I should care more, so I say, "that must be hard, yes, that's got to be hard…"

"It's weird," Clara says. "It's obviously harder to be homeless and… well, mentally ill and living on the streets, but everything got so much harder for me so fast and I am. Not. Coping."

I take a deep breath and look over to Lexi, who looks back at me with a thought not spoken. I look back to Clara. "We're going to get you home," I say, turning to Lexi and nodding. Lexi offers me a soft smile.

"You know, Maddox, I admire you," Lexi says after a moment of silence. "You want to go all the way to the Canadian border to help someone get home. That's really nice of you, I guess."

Lexi's kind, as I said, and she brings me a smile. "Thank you, thank you, I want to be kind like you when it all goes bad."

She smiles softly even as Clara looks at me as though I am doing something wrong. She doesn't say anything this time, but she refuses to be too close to me as I lead the two of them down the road. It's me, with a torch, in the darkness, and two ghosts in the black void following the light like moths.

"How should we get to the border?" I ask them both; "walking is slow."

"I don't know," Clara says first, skipping up a little closer to me. "I don't mind however long it takes."

"If you want to get to the border quickly, a bike would at least be faster," Lexi suggests; she's still in the darkness behind me. "I'm sure stores would still have them. If this really is the apocalypse like everyone's saying I think we're justified in just going in and taking them."

"It's not the apocalypse." The idea tightens my chest. "We're still here."

"I didn't say it was the apocalypse-" Clara starts to say, but Lexi drowns her out.

"It's been the apocalypse for us for ages, Maddox," she says, "now it's just the apocalypse for everyone else. And that's... what you're seeing, I think."

"-Oh. You're talking to her." Clara sounds almost disappointed in me and it twinges at my heart again.

I'm being nice to her, being kind like Lexi, and she sounds like she's almost scared of me because of Lexi. "Well, does... she... at least have any ideas?"

"Bikes," I tell Clara, "we'll go get bikes."

"Okay," both she and Lexi say; Clara adds, "from where?"

"It's not the apocalypse," I say to Lexi, "but can we still get them from a store? Without paying?"

"Why are you asking me?" Clara says even though I'm not.

"I don't see why not," Lexi says. "I mean, looting has started already, hasn't it? What's two more people looting?"

"What's two more people looting?" I say to Clara, taking Lexi at her word. I trust her with some decisions when she trusts me with some. We are a team. "Let's go."

"This way," Lexi says, taking steps ahead of me and leading me along the main road. All is silent on the streets, everyone huddled inside once all has ended. It has not ended, because this is not the apocalypse and for Lexi and I nothing has changed. If Clara doesn't get home, she can be part of our team and things will be fine for her too, as long as she isn't rude to Lexi anymore. Lexi is too kind for anyone to be rude to her. If everything is still fine for us it can be fine for almost anyone.

"Are you really okay with just... looting? I mean, if we want to keep society together, we can't just do whatever we want like it's already fallen apart." Clara's close at my elbow again like she suddenly doesn't mind. "My mother's probably got to deal with everyone breaking the law and all because of this. It's a natural disaster, really."

"I don't know how I feel about looting," I say, and the uncertainty underlines my voice. "Is this a natural disaster? Society falling apart?"

"You're cute, Maddox, but here's the thing," Lexi says as Clara quietly ponders my words. "Society is everyone and if it's already being done, we're not really making anything worse. That's how I'm going to look at it. And a natural disaster? I guess it depends if it's natural, I don't know."

"It's a natural disaster," Clara says. "I don't want to steal anything, but..."

"Here." Lexi says it just as I look at the big sign, the department store that used to always have lights on every hour of the night. They're closed now, always. The front window is already smashed in and the glass glitters in the firelight as we walk closer; Lexi walks carelessly across the shards even with the thinness of her shoes, and Clara has no issue crossing them at all. I am careful not to drive glass deep into my foot. Lexi and Clara both go to the broken window, but I try the door and find it is not locked.

"Oh," Clara says when I push the door open, "I didn't realise. I was just going to climb through the window like an idiot."

Lexi laughs a little under her breath as she follows me, Clara behind her, a bit more hesitant. The firelight lights up shelves of things that were once new, sculpted or welded or glued or stitched together, now in pieces of clay or metal or plastic or yarn across the floor. Most shelves are empty. I knew food had been stolen already because Lexi and I had been here the second day after power disappeared, and I was as uncertain as I am now, but I followed Lexi, as I do now. We had seen bikes then but much more has been stolen since that time.

I know where to go, and Lexi and Clara follow me. "How do you know where you're going?" Clara asks, skipping alongside Lexi. Does she know she's right next to her?

"We were here before," I tell her.

"I know," Lexi says.

At the same time Clara scoffs, "we, you mean, you and the girl that doesn't exist?"

"Stop saying Lexi doesn't exist." I scratch at a bug on my hand and when I turn around Lexi's smiling at me, kind of sadly but it's still a smile and I'll take it. "I don't like it."

"Jesus, sorry. I just hope you're aware that she doesn't." Listening to Clara talk like that is upsetting, and I grit my teeth in what must be anger. "Look, just. Where are the bikes? This darkness is super unsettling."

The darkness doesn't bother me, and Lexi doesn't seem to mind either. It's been dark for eighteen days.

"Here." I turn into the part of the store Lexi and I saw them in. "Should be here. Should be…"

The firelight in the darkness is a stain of orange across the dark cloth, and there's a lump in the cloth that shouldn't be there. A man stands up, holding a bike, and looks me up and down, suspicion oozing from him. I look at him and feel he cannot be trusted totally but can be trusted for now. "What do you want?" he asks, and I don't recognise him, but I know he might fight. Instinctively, I back up in front of Lexi and keep myself between him and her; she's too kind to get hurt. Clara falls behind me naturally. I will protect them both.

"We need bikes," I say simply. My voice comes out empty as it sometimes does. "How many are there?"

"There's three left, and I need one." The man's wary but reasonable. Kind enough. "Is it just the two of you?"

"We need three," I begin, but both girls protest that.

"No, we just need two," Clara says to the man, "ignore John, he's got issues."

"Maddox, don't worry about it," Lexi says, her hand at my elbow as she feels my hesitation. "Just get two, okay? I guess… Clara? Is that her name? Her and I can share."

It's a case of Lexi's kindness making me trust her. I let her decision go, let it become reality. "Okay," I say to the man, "we will take two."

The man looks at me strangely again. "Alright. I don't want no trouble." He backs up, back into the darkness, where he fades in with the walls and only a thin line of firelight grounds him in the reality nearby. "Best of luck to you, alright?"

He begins to walk away, wheeling the bike along, a fading noise of clicking in the darkness. I turn to Clara and Lexi, and Lexi smiles softly at me. "I'm glad that went well," she says, gesturing to the two bikes that remain. "Let's just take them and go."

Clara breathes a sigh of relief. "Oh, thank god. Let's take the bikes and go."

I keep the torch in one hand and pull a bike up with the other hand. I'm walking back through the aisle before I turn and look, and I see both Clara and Lexi walking a bike alongside them in the darkness. It's a break in the fabric of reality, a fabric which has been dark for quite a long time, dark for the rest of the world for weeks now. I close my eyes, hoping that when I open them the break will be repaired, but it is not. Both Clara and Lexi hold a bike.

I ignore the unsettling feeling that has wrapped around my heart now, knowing that reality will, eventually, iron itself out; Lexi always tells me not to worry about what is and is not real, because it stresses me, and I lash out. I know that not everything I see is real. I know that, and that is why it hurts when Clara tells me Lexi is not real, because I'm scared she's correct.

"You're real, aren't you, Lexi?" I ask, and the short silence that follows the question aches like pins in my heart.

She laughs a little bit, a soft, kind laugh. Kind, that's how I've always known her and how I always will. "Of course I am," she says. "You're fine, Maddox, okay? We've talked about this."

"Clara, is she real?"

"No, but you keep telling me not to mention that." Clara's annoyance bites at me. I want to bite back, but Lexi's kindness has helped me to stop, as I try to be kinder to others; she wouldn't want me to be mean to Clara, whether she's real or not, and so I don't.

I scratch at a bug on my hand, and the darkness seems to press in, fighting against the firelight as a force to be reckoned with. It has won against the rest of the world, but it has yet to win against me.

"Do you think we should check the rest of this before we go?" Lexi asks as we walk our bikes towards the front. "Can there be much left?"

"There will be little," I say to her, "and we looked already. The food is all gone, and what else is there?"

"Are you talking to her again?" Clara asks and I ignore her. Her voice grates. I am doing her a nice thing and she's being rude to and about Lexi, and I wonder why I'm even being nice to her when people like her were never once nice to me. The daughters of government officials do not care for people like Lexi and I, so why am I caring for her?

"You know, this whole… power loss was honestly a good thing for us," Lexi says, "because when everyone's losing so much, they freak out and leave so much behind that we can just… have."

"You're right, Lexi." I turn and look Clara in the eyes, daggers from my irises; if she will not be kind, she can't come with us. We'll return to the safe crack in the alleyway and she can find her own way home.

"Don't look at me like that," Clara's voice is suddenly afraid and guilt twists in my heart, and I turn away from her, even as she says, "I'm sorry, I'm not trying to judge you or anything, okay? Let's just go. You're doing me a favour and I should be grateful for that."

"Yes," is all I have to say as I push the doors open again. I cannot ride and hold the torch at the same time, and so I snuff it out. Clara gasps as the darkness envelops us again, but Lexi and I are used to this. Out on the street, we mount the bikes, and the starlight guides Clara to follow us.

"Which way is it?" Clara asks, and I look up to the sky. The moon is still a silent watcher, but she knows me, and beside her are the stars that point the way, brighter in the night sky than ever before now that light from the earth doesn't drown them out. If I had to guess I would know that the moon did this, because we did not appreciate her stars enough; we grew too self-confident and tried to build our own stars, forgetting where we came from.

"Maddox, which way?" Lexi asks as I'm silent in the wake of Clara's question.

"This," I tell them, taking the path the stars guide me in. My father taught me this a long time ago- which star leads north. From there I know south. South-south-east, Ambassador Bridge, I know this, and I know how to lead them there. We're going to get Clara home.

The road is not empty. I see people skulking away from us in the night, and deep in the dark streets orange lights can be seen, the fires forming stars on earth. The moonlight is all we need to find our way, and we are crossed by no one. The silence, silent compared to the gentle noise from before the blackout, pushes in, dampens everything. When the world is silent it is difficult to make noise, difficult to make a sound. All the trees have fallen now, and they may've made a sound, but they make no sound anymore.

"Is it far?" Lexi asks. "Do you think we'll actually be able to cross the border?"

"Not far," I tell her; I'm as certain as I can be without knowing. I know the streets well enough, not this part of town, but I know how to get there. Lexi has never been great with directions, always trusting me. I trust her and she trusts me and it itches at me that Clara says she isn't real. "I don't know if we'll be able to cross the border. Clara will."

"I can't imagine why I wouldn't be," Clara says. "I'm not even sure there'll be border forces, right? Everything's chaos right now, don't you think they'll care more about other things?"

"I don't know, I don't," I say; the way the pedals move under my feet makes me feel off balance. I'm not off balance. "Lexi, will there be border forces?"

"Well, I was asking you," Lexi says, and there's a smile in her voice that spreads to me. "I think so. But if there is, we can just turn back, Maddox. Or maybe find somewhere along the river to stay? You suggested that a few weeks ago."

"I don't remember," I say, "but I think it's a good idea."

"What is?" Clara asks from behind me, calling loud in the silent night.

"The river. If we can't get across the border."

"We can get across the border," Clara says, sounding certain. "Or at least I can."

"We don't have to cross the border," Lexi says. Her words overlap Clara's.

"We don't," I admit, "we just have to get Clara there."

"What- oh." Clara's response is sharp and short. "Are we nearly there?"

"Yeah," I say before I know, but if I read the signs correctly in the dark it is true. Fires prick through the dark far ahead. "Almost there."

The moon lights our way, and the shadows of her light dance around our feet, cycling alongside us; I can hear a distant whisper of her voice, not loud enough to make out the words, and I close my eyes to listen. I open them when I lose my balance and the sound of her voice is lost.

"Hey. Stop."

That is not her voice. The fires are still a while ahead, and the man who steps out in front of us holds no torch. He is difficult to make out from shadow, his dark uniform masking him. I stop even though I do not want to, turning to Lexi for guidance.

The man looks to me, not to either of them. His hand lays uneasily on his hip. "Where do you think you're going?"

I see him and I know he is not kind, and I do not trust him. Anxiety and knowledge of this locks up my throat. "I-I- we're- we're crossing the border- we're- I'm taking her to Canada, I'm-"

"Nobody's to come in or out, regardless of who they are or why," he says, skeptical eyebrows raising at my shaky voice. The girls come up on my left, each wheeling a bike beside them, and I turn, hoping one of them will speak, if one of them can.

"Maddox," Lexi says softly, "let's go."

"I have beyond good reason," Clara says, stepping up and showing herself. "If you don't allow me to cross, you'll be in trouble you can't comprehend."

"She's- she's the daughter of a senator. Canadian senator. You have to let her through, let her through," I say, struggling to keep each word even and ironed out.

The guard looks to my left, eyebrows raising again. He does not trust me, and his eyes glitter in the dark, and I do not trust him, he wants to hurt us. "Is this true, ma'am? Because I still don't think..."

He keeps talking despite Clara's interruption, but her voice is louder than his. She seems to stand in more light than he does; her face is clear, like the moon is highlighting her to me. The moonlight seems to grow brighter around her. "Just let me through or you will be sorry."

"It's not true," Lexi says quietly. I hear her voice, and my head's beginning to ache. I can hear the moon now; she's just softly calling my name, but it's louder than anything else now. "Maddox, come on."

"Maddox, is that your name?" The guard's eyes are daggers filled with venom; maybe not intentionally, but I feel it deep in my veins. John, John, John, the moon is saying; every word seems to hurt despite how loud it isn't. "I don't care why you came here now, but you and your friend are going to have to leave."

"I told you," Clara begins to sound desperate, stepping up towards the man and getting into his face. She looks small against his form and he takes no notice of her. "I'm not leaving, and if you don't let me through, you'll regret it."

John, the moon says, she is being mean to him, isn't she? She's the kind of person who never would've helped you. Yet you helped her.

"Just let Clara through," I say weakly, searching around me desperately for a purpose that I am meant to be following. The words I can hear whispered against my ears hurt; they make me think I do the wrong thing. I step up to the man and he backs up, stiffening in his stance, pointing at me with two hands raised together, a dark shape in them; I cannot trust him. My eyes fall and my voice stutters through, lapsing every word. He holds a gun. "Just- her- just- please, let-"

Society is collapsing, the moon says. Let it collapse. It let you collapse.

"What's your name, ma'am? Clara?" the guard says, as Lexi comes to my side to hold me up. She holds me up where Clara does not, and Clara turns to face me, glaring like it's my fault I brought her here when it's exactly what she wanted, it's exactly what she wanted and I did it and it's not my fault he won't listen to me. It's not my fault.

"No, Lexi," answers she, at the exact same moment as Clara answers, "yes, Clara," and the moon's rays seem to almost hurt, blinding me even as the darkness doesn't allow me to see. I scratch at a bug on my hand and the rays seem to only increase; I hide my eyes behind my hands and groan at the noise of the moon whispering wordless things against the nape of my neck. John, John, John, the moon whispers, and I whisper back, silent; I got Clara to the border, didn't I? I did the good thing?

"Lexi, you seem rational," the guard says, and reality is cracking. It is impossible to describe the burn of reality disconnecting, struggling to make sense. "Can you convince your friend here to step away, please? It's my duty to stop anyone from crossing this bridge."

"Are you just going to ignore me?" Clara yells, and I can hear her stomping on the concrete. I focus not on that but Lexi's hands around my shoulders; the moon guides her, and I trust her, and with her I fall to my knees, reaching through the burn to find reality. The moon keeps whispering my name.

"Give me a minute," Lexi tells the guard, before she speaks to me. I feel the asphalt under my fingers. "Maddox, listen to me. You did a good thing, okay? The world's falling apart and there's nothing you can do and you wanted to be the one to fix that. That's great, Maddox, alright? You're doing great. But we've got to go now, okay? We're going to go to the riverside, we'll find a nice place to stay there for a while, and everything's going to be okay. You and I are going to be okay."

"And Clara?" The moon quiets down once Lexi starts talking. I listen for Lexi's voice instead of hers.

"She'll be fine," Lexi says, taking my hand to lift me to my feet. Both of our hands are dirty and rough; I look down at my palms in what moonlight I'm given and see them dry. I turn to look at the guard and try to smile at him, even though he does not smile back.

"The river sounds good," I say to Lexi, staring at the guard, wondering if he's real. "I could… wash my hands."

"Don't just leave me here."

I hear Clara's voice, but I don't see her. In the darkness, the void has enveloped her, and there's nothing to be seen at all. I saw the tree fall, and it was a sapling that I could lift and replant; and I fear that leaving her alone means she will simply fall again, like every other tree has done, joining me and Lexi on the forest floor, silent and unheard as we were.

"Clara," I whisper, barely loud enough for my own ears to catch it. Lexi does not hear me.

"Thank you, officer," Lexi says, retrieving her bike from the two that have fallen to the ground. "I'm sorry about my friend."

The officer nods his head and does not answer her. Distrustfully, I take up my bike as well, turning to the moon for answers; Lexi has laid a calm upon me, and the moon is silent now, hiding behind cloud.

"I-" I don't know what I want Lexi to know, but I want her to know something. She waits patiently for me. I turn one last time, looking for Clara in the darkness, and I see nothing, although I feel ill at ease, waiting for her to return from the darkness any moment. "Lexi, did I... did we do something wrong, going here? Going here, should we have stayed?"

"Should we have stayed?" Lexi clarifies, and my nod makes her think. "I don't know, Maddox. I know you wanted to do a good thing, and I wanted to see you happy. Besides, I kind of..." her shrug gives something away, but I cannot name it. "...I don't know. I wanted to move. Let's camp by the river, yeah?"

"Yeah." My backpack is heavy on my shoulders. When I look up to the moon, she is silent. She speaks through Lexi.

"To the river, then, Maddox. We'll be fine."

IT SNOWS HERE

BY JUSTIN ALCALA

DAY 65

'**I**'m ugly. I was born ugly and will always be ugly — a life without potential. It's not that I have large ears for a boy or that my head is a bit too round. No, I am what happens when nature gets careless. It's called Neurofibromatosis, a rare condition that shows off its unpleasantries from the outside-in. Tumors along my spinal cord have hunched my back, disfigured my hands and turned my face into a mask of melting wax.

Dad used to say warthogs are ugly too, but the other animals don't have the balls to tell it to the pig's face. Dad grew up in the city. It hardened his heart almost as much as his knuckles. Mom was the opposite. She loved to tell me as a boy that even the unseemliest weed grows a beautiful flower. She always had a way of making everything better.

Even before the darkness, I lived in the shadows. I didn't go outside. I never made friends. My only company were my parents and my books. Mom says I read more each week than she had in her lifetime. Books help me escape. They teach me lessons. They make me laugh. When I was away with tutors or physicians, I ached for my books. They were all I needed.

It was just another day when the power went out. Mom had taken me to my appointment for chest pain management. When doctors weren't pretending my presence was bearable, they poked, prodded and ran me through every machine in the building. After a full day of the gamut, the men and women in lab coats asked Mom if they could have a word with her in private. I knew that the worst, the fate my doctors had warned us about at a young age, was looming. My short time here had run out. At least I'd made it to seventeen.

As I waited on the table with wax-paper that stuck to my toadish skin, the lights flickered. A low hum rumbled through the walls, then everything went black. I called for Mom who raced in the room, her face shadowed behind her phone light. She tried to stretch her arms around my gigantic body.

"Not to worry," she comforted with a squeeze. "It's just a power outage. It should be back on in a moment." Her cheeks were damp.

The hospital's generators kicked in and the lights turned back on. For once, I noticed, the staff and visitors weren't staring at me. They were too busy bumbling with phones, gawping out windows and hurrying to gather their things. Panic colored their faces. Our doctor told us we'd need to reconvene another time, and, shortly after, Mom gathered her purse from the checkup room, we left.

As we piled into the car, I noticed fires from distant neighborhoods along the horizon. The highway was black except for the few headlights from speeding cars, and although Mom cursed the frantic drivers, calling them broken lunatics, raving demons and other Dr. Suess like titles, we made it home safe. For the rest of that night, we waited by the window for Dad to come home and the power to turn back on. Neither returned.

One day became two, two days stretched into a week, and a week into months. Autumn surrendered its post to winter as rain hardened into snow. Mom tried to cry in other rooms, but I knew she was sad. Dad's disappearance wore on us all, but I was used to the loneliness. Mom had friends before the blackout. She had Dad. She had me. The solitude was a stranger to her all these years.

We lived in a place where the sun only visited on weekends, and even in the morning, darkness complicated things. We stayed in one room. Our heat came from hoarded Kenosha Times burned in a tin wastebasket and our water flowed from our backyard's koi pond. We'd gone through all of our food, even the decade old preserves in the basement, but the grocers never reopened. Mom heard our neighbors foraged what little gas remained in town and drove south before winter. So occasionally she'd rummage through vacant homes and come back with an abandoned can of condensed milk or a box Italian breadcrumbs. I kept myself busy as I always had with books by the window while she was gone.

Someone told Mom the cities were war zones, but our town was too old for any of that. It moved slowly even in the face of calamity. It's not to say it wouldn't happen someday. Going tribal was just too *avant-garde* for the locals. They were too conventional to get caught up in the hoopla. So whenever Mom went out, I wasn't too worried.

As days passed, I tried ignoring the ache in my chest, but it was becoming unbearable. I slept sitting up, which strangely eased the pain. Still, I realized it wouldn't be long now before Mom tried to wake me and my eyes wouldn't open. Then one day Mom flipped the tables. The dawn sunlight nudged me awake, but Mom didn't stir as usual. When I checked on her, she was shivering in bed. She'd lost all color, her sheets were damp and she couldn't swallow. I didn't know what to do.

Caring for her for the next few weeks kept me busy, but as she regained her strength, her appetite grew. Our pantry was barren and all the jars were licked clean. If I wanted her to get better, I'd need to go into the cold. This presented a problem. I learned long ago I frightened people. With law eroded, I worried someone might see me and react out of impulse. For that reason, I covered up in my hoodie, donned a pair of Dad's snow goggles and topped it off with the puffiest winter jacket in the house. I wrapped my face in a scarf for good measure and left.

People who aren't from the North think winter is deadliest when there're blizzards and snowstorms. If only this were true. The cruelest winters come from the quietly bleak days when the frigid air drains the life out of everything. If you saw it in a photo, you might not imagine dead birds perched in nests and fish swam frozen in lakes. You might not know about the winds that bit through walls, frosting anything out of fire's reach. Today was one of those days.

I crushed the ice with Dad's tight boots. A trim of snow festooned every roof, fence and tree branch like some halcyon Christmas card. My nose ran, even with a scarf over it, and I immediately had to pee. *Dang it.* I pressed on regardless. Luckily, it didn't take me long to get to the town's central square, and as I passed by the banks and shops, I noticed my favorite bookstore had a sign in front of their door.

It read, "It is a far, far better thing that I do, than I have ever done; it is a far, far better rest that I go to than I have ever known. -Sydney Carton, A Tale of Two Cities." Underneath in blue sharpie the writing added, "Gone for good. Take any book you'd like."

I tried the brass knob with a twist and shove. The door opened. Even though a clear invitation permitted me in, taking that first step still seemed wrong. The store greeted me with a creek of its floorboards as I moved towards my favorite section. I freed my face of my scarf and goggles so I could better read the titles. The store still smelled of old paper. I looked over the fantasy shelves, eerie in the moonlight shining through tinted blue glass. I remember the first time my Mom had taken me here. The old man, who never introduced himself, was one of the few people on a very short list who never batted an eye when he saw me. That simple act forged this store as one of the few places I felt safe visiting in public, if not briefly.

I sailed between the dozen long bookshelves making prudent selections. I ignored the nonfiction section, which still displayed titles about political shrewdness and celebrity cooking, stopping once I'd made it to the science fiction area.

I'd read most of the novels from cover to back, but there were still a few that were strangers to me. I grabbed three hardcovers, thanked the store with a glance, and then made my way back out. It was a nice break, but I had to remember why I was out. Mom starved at home.

Mom once told me most of the houses she explored had left little, but she was reluctant to go into complete strangers' homes so flippantly. There were two places in particular I knew she wouldn't explore, The Kelly's Gas Station and the windmill house. The Kellys were a family that owned a gas station by the highway and had been part of the town since it dropped its first stones. They were tight knit and feared by most locals. Their ruddy gas station nestled along our town's lone highway and catered to travelers unaware of the Kellys' spotty reputation.

The windmill house is just what Mom called it. It was an ordinary house, mostly with the addition of solar panels on its roof and a miniature turbine posted along its yard. A family from the city had just recently moved in. No one really knew them, but then again, no one really knew me either. Perhaps that's how they liked it.

Both places were on the other side of town across from the highway. I continued my trek through the square, glimpsing in stores whose window weren't frosted. There likely wouldn't be any food, but it didn't stop me from looking. However, as I huffed on the glass of the Mexican restaurant, I heard snow crushing at a fast pace on the corner of my block. They were short and steady footsteps. I pulled the scarf back over my swollen lips and searched for the source.

A girl or perhaps a woman of average height made her way to me. She had long silver and purple dyed hair pouring from a stocking hat, a peacoat and one of those knitted rainbow scarfs that only look good on mannequins. Her pants were form fitting, made from the stuff that astronauts use, which made her look top heavy. She wore combat boots and held a book in her hands; I think Andrew

Smith. Most terrifying, as I took in her face with pierced nose and lip, I noticed for the first time that she was pretty.

Her face was fixed in surprise and she hesitated as she held her book to her chest. The pair of us exchanged glances. She stared at me as if my full set of winter ninja clothing was invisible. I didn't know what to do. Then she violated me with the most aggressive act of all.

"Hey," she nodded while sniffing snot back up from her pierced nostril. I smelled strawberry perfume in the cold air. I tried to straighten my crooked back, which felt unnatural, like bending your knee in reverse.

"Um, hey," I responded. It was all I could muster. She looked at the books in my hands, her mascara painted eyes widening. She'd caught me stealing. Scared, I covered the novels with my ski gloves.

"Morgenstern, huh?" she asked matter-of-factly.

"Uh," I lifted *The Night Circus* and shrugged. "Yeah. I uh, I heard that it's good."

"It is."

"Oh, uh, I took it from the bookstore. You don't mind that I take it."

"No."

"Um, thanks." I turned backwards towards the bookstore as if it would give me evidence or argumentative support. "The sign said take any book you like."

"Yeah, I know. I'm returning this one and getting another."

"Returning?"

"Yeah," she shrugged. "I mean, I get that I don't really have to, but it makes it feel like a library. There's no damn library in this town."

"It's the worst," I blabbed subconsciously. I froze in place. *Why did I say that?*

"Yeah, I know," She snickered. "Well, going to the bookstore at least kind of reminds me of real life. Well, not to say that life was real before this."

How long could I keep this charade up? It seemed as if at any moment this girl, this beautiful girl, would see through me. Maybe she'd unmask me like the Phantom of the Opera or perhaps reality would slowly dissolve into her conscience and she'd spin around and sprint as she screamed. I tried to calm myself, taking even breaths through my scarf.

"I'm Averie," she waved.

"Uh, Averie."

"You're Averie too?" she smirked.

"No, uh, no, I'm not." I stuttered. "Sam."

"Like Samwise Gamgee."

"Yeah," I fake chuckled, "he's the worst."

"What? I love Tolkien."

"Oh yeah, uh, me too. I'm a big Lord of the Rings fan. Love me some Samwise."

Her smirk stretched into a smile. I wanted to dive through the Mexican restaurant's window. My chest tightened. This was too much. I needed an out.

"So," she shrugged, "it's pretty cold tonight. Why so late Sam?"

My thoughts raced back to my Mom. "Food," I fretted. All at once reality kicked in. "Oh, no, I need food. Um, Averie, it was real nice to meet you, but it's my Mom. She's sick and I'm supposed to get her food."

"I have food."

"You do?"

"Well," she bit at the brass ring around her lip, "I mean not here. We have a big storage pantry at home. If you walk with me, I'm sure we can spare some."

"What? Uh."

It was the mention of *we* and *walk with me* and everything else in the package that gave me goosebumps. Why, after all these years, did it take the face of Armageddon and a heart held together by glue for me to have any regular conversation with someone? I couldn't cope, so in an act of defiance I mustered up the courage to stop Averie in her tracks.

"Sure, yeah," I thanked. "That'd be great." *Long live the resistance.*

"Cool," she tucked her bright bang behind her ear. "Mind if I return this book first?"

"Uh, yeah." I rubbed the back of my neck. "I mean, no I uh, I don't mind."

"Sweet. Come on."

Averie took a moment to trade out novels back at the bookstore. She enjoyed the same authors as me, from Anne Rice and Christopher Moore. When she finished, she straightened up the shop before closing up. She led us across town from there. My Dad used to complain that it was a shame I'd been born sick, as I was big enough to be an NFL linebacker. I wondered if Averie felt safer with me around, but my conscience told me that my suspicion was based out of fear. She never asked me to show my face. She never asked me why I was limping. She said nothing at all. That is until we reached Highway 50.

The road that divided the heart of town from Kelly's Gas Station was a two-lane disaster filled with nothing at all. Most people passing through ignored our neighborhood for good reason. It was small and there was little to offer compared to other communities, nothing besides Kelly's Gas Station. The two pump convenient store refused to move on from its early 90s pastel paint, chipped from wear. It had a black shoveled lot with tired yellow stripes that wrapped around the store, and a single mechanic's garage door that no one brought their car to due to the Kelly's reputation. Mom tried to shelter me from just how bad the Kellys were, but twice we'd drove home from the hospital to find police parked outside the station.

I narrowed my eyes at the building. A crooked cardboard sign along the entrance read *No More Gas* in big letters, duct taped just above a Confederate flag decal. Three bullet holes patched with flattened Twinkie boxes pierced beneath. Below the door, a trail of red dots moved away from the station, pooling like a welcome mat along the single cement step. Both gas pumps had their nozzles removed from the hoses. I tried to look for any signs of people, but all I found was a life-size Marlboro man advertisement leanly coolly along the wall near the rusty air tank.

I was hesitant to cross through the Kellys' gas station. Before I could object, Averie looked both ways along the caked highway and took a step forward. I grabbed at her shoulder out of impulse, pulling my hand back once I'd realized what I'd done. I sunk in place. Averie didn't seem to care. She tilted her head like a dog listening to a whistle.

"What's wrong?" she asked, her breath pluming with steam.

"Look," I pointed at the door. I watched as Averie's gaze traveled to the entrance before her eyes went wide.

"Huh. I didn't notice that before. You don't think that is what it looks like, do you?"

I shrugged.

"Could it be transmission fluid?" she asked.

"Uh, I'm not sure. Maybe."

Averie crossed her arms. "Guess we can go around if you want."

"Um, Averie," I mirrored her stance, hiding my hands under my armpits, "where exactly do you live?"

"Oh," her head cocked back. "Yeah, duh. I live on Pulaski Street near the lake." There was only one house on that street. I took a second glance at the highway and noticed a pair of footprints matching Averie's traveling from the other side. She'd walked this way before.

"Uh, you live in the windmill house?"

"Yeah, how'd you know?"

"Oh uh, it's a small town."

"Never heard it called that, but yeah."

"Wait," I hesitated, "do you have power?"

"I wish," she sighed. "You still need the grid. My dad says we could get it if we had a little juice, but it looks like the power plant won't be back in business soon."

I laugh-snorted as I thought about our route, peering along the roadside. Pulaski Street, which stretched behind the gas station, hadn't been shoveled. Icicles clung to the street post which protruded from the half foot of snow. If we used the station's shoveled blacktop, we'd save ourselves a few minutes and a lot of energy. My feet were already numb.

"Well, if we don't cut through here, it's a mile out of our way. I guess, uh, just be careful."

"It's cool. I haven't had a problem yet."

"Okay, uh, cool."

We crossed the highway onto Kelly's gas station, cutting through the parking lot towards Pulaski Street. The station sign hung on rusted chains that creaked with the draft. I tried to be calm but felt uneasy. My eyes locked onto the property during our short trip, and we'd nearly crossed without issue when I spotted it. At the back of the building was a gas generator. I tapped Averie on the shoulder and pointed, clearing my hoarse throat.

"You think that'd be enough juice to get your solar panels going again?" I inquired.

"Whoa, no way," Averie boldly walked over, "let's go see."

"Uh, Averie, wait." But she didn't wait. Averie double backed and brushed the snow off the generator's logo with her glove. I hurried to catch up as she read the label. Unlike most of Kelly's station, the generator appeared to be relatively new. Averie bit at her gloved finger, studying the energy converting machine.

"You know what, Sam? This could work."

"Really?"

"Yeah, really. Nice work."

"Oh, uh, thanks." My chest still ached, but for a moment, a rush of warmth spilled over me. Mom gave me compliments all of the time, but besides that, praise was rare. It was nice.

"I mean," she looked at a chord dangling from the generator's top, "if we figured out how to plug this into the house, it would only take a little gas and we could have a powered the place up again. Do you get what that would mean Sam?" Averie didn't give me time to respond. "Dad bought the house because he wanted to escape," Averie made air quotes as she deepened her voice, "big city costs." She furrowed a brow at the flat tire on the bottom of the industrial yellow machine. "Everything in that house is electric. It would mean heat again. It would mean lights and warm water. I mean, we could survive."

"Uh, wow."

"Yeah *wow*, Sam. We might be able to take in people from town. You and your Mom should be the first ones, well, if she'd be cool with that."

I thought about how nice it would be to have heat for Mom. Before I finished that idea, a clamor came from inside the station. Someone dropped a box of tools or utensils. Averie's broad eyes stared at me.

"Let's get out of here," she whispered. I nodded while scanning the lot. There were still no signs of life.

We ran off towards Pulaski. I looked over my shoulder several times as we distanced ourselves from the station. During one of my last glance overs, I recognized the distinct orange glow from a lantern flickering inside the station. The building lit up as if it were a Jack-o'-lantern. I stopped to watch. Someone inside the Kelly's Station blocked the light in its back window, creating a shadow that stood inside. They were now watching us as we made our way to Averie's house.

As we continued down the street, the sky opened, letting snow escape the clouds. It was a soft drift, the sort that hypnotized you with its beauty and caused you to let down your guard. Make no mistake though, it was just as frigid as any other storm.

My body tightened up as a light gale tiptoed through Pulaski Street. Averie must have felt it too because her body shivered. I wondered what her skin felt like if I touched it but reminded myself that eventually I'd have to abandon our lovely accord. Luckily, as we retraced the last of Averie's old footsteps, I could make out her strange home ahead.

It was a modern house with a roof slanted like a beret, windows large enough for a greenhouse and a smoking chimney. Solar panels crowed the roof. They looked as if giant legos secured themselves on shingles. Along the front yard near a stack of tarp-covered wood was an eco-friendly car parked next to a tall pole with a three bladed turbine faintly spinning like a pinwheel. A bearded man in winter attire balanced atop of a ladder with a broom, brushing off the roof and walls.

"Dad, you will not believe this," Averie called out, running ahead. "We found a generator." Averie's father took his climb climbing down the ladder rungs. I wondered if this would be a good time to melt into the background and leave, but before I could retreat, Averie's father cleared his throat.

"Who's this?" Averie's father asked while removing his clouded glasses and wiping them with his coat sleeve. Averie looked over her shoulders and smiled.

"That's Sam," she said simply, "He's cool. He reads books."

For the first time, I didn't hear my name as Sam the big ugly kid, Sam the sick boy, Sam the freak. I was Sam. I was cool. I read books.

"Hi Sam," Averie's father nodded as he scaled down the ladder.

"Uh, hey," I waved.

"We need to give Sam food for his Mom," Averie explained. "She's sick. But first Sam needs to warm up."

"Oh, I uh, I'm good," I held out my gloved hands and shook my head. "I should go."

Averie kicked up snow as she slogged towards me. She grabbed my hand and tugged. I panicked, and although I was big enough to toss her over my shoulder, I delicately pulled my hand away before she recognized any misshapen parts underneath.

"Come on," she demanded, "I can show you my books."

Before I realized what was even going on, Averie was pulling me as if I were a leashed dog. I followed her and her father into the red door to their house. Even without power, the place was nice. The front room had porcelain floors with a beige couch and ivory walls. A ribbon fireplace danced across a dozen logs. I delighted in the hoarded heat from the small breaks in my winter armor and smelled the aroma of burning wood. I stood huddled, hands locked together as my posture bowed. Averie whispered something into her father's ear, smiled, and then patted him on the shoulder. Averie's father gave a pursed smile. For the first time I noticed how small he was compared to my trollish body.

"Dad is gonna bag up food for you," Averie informed me as she shed her coat. She wore a black long-sleeved Misfits skull shirt underneath. As I took it in, my mind turned all toad like and noticed her breasts. I closed my eyes immediately and shook my head like a child trying to disbelieve a closet monster. *Perhaps I was the monster?* Now more than ever I felt it both inside and out. Averie didn't seem to notice any of it.

"Let's go," she grabbed at my jacket. "You need to see my books."

"No, no," I conjured up any lie within arm's reach, "I need to get back to Mom. If I take everything off, it'll take forever to put it all back on."

"It'll just take a second," she insisted. "No need to take anything off."

I found it odd that she let a person dressed like the Invisible Man remain faceless, but as I stamped snow onto the steps leading to her room, I was blindsided by everything that made up Averie. Beyond the band posters, bookshelves and framed photographs in her room were canvases, at least a dozen, covered in freshly painted art. There were murals of Pulaski Street, depictions of a big city with no power and a grey winter landscape. Most spectacular, near the corner of her room was a portrait of a bright haired girl in the arms of a familiar father. Along the edge of the canvas, a somber woman watched them from some great divide. It galvanized dead memories of my own father, memories I'd ignored out of a need to survive.

"Well, what do you think?" she questioned while leaning on a vanity to unlace her boots.

"Uh, wow," I spluttered, "it's really good. I mean, it's great." *It really was.*

"Thanks."

"How long do these take to paint?"

"Depends," she shrugged. "Sometimes, it's days. Once in a while though, the paint just flows off of the brush. Like this one." She moved over to a parade of children lined like sunflowers in a field, sunbathing in a clouded dawn. "I did this in a day. It helps pass the time."

Every painting showed me something different, a window to Averie's thoughts. I'd only just met her, but she was special. It made me wonder if I could preserve this relationship until my heart gave out. That would be nice. Perhaps if there were phones or even mail, but without it, hope was thin.

"Well, you're really talented," I rasped as the blood in my toes returned. "Hey, uh, I should go."

"Cool. First, I owe you books."

"Uh, no, you don't owe me anything."

"Think of it as a way to get you to come back."

Averie picked out a handful of paperbacks to add to the ones I'd taken from the bookstore and then guided me down the stairs where her dad was waiting. He had a chartreuse reusable grocery bag filled with cans and plastic containers. It looked as if it could feed us for days.

"Uh," I stammered, "I can't take this."

"Yes you can," Averie protested, taking the bag from her Dad's hand and shoving it in my chest. "It's the least we can do. You helped me get home safely. Plus, you found that generator. We're cool now."

I grinned behind my scarf. "Can I, uh, repay you?"

"Not unless you can rewire an inverter," Averie's Dad chuckled.

I thought about it. "Probably," I shrugged. "Well, uh, if I could read up on it first."

"Hmm," Averie's Dad's expression sobered. He cleared his throat. "Follow me."

Averie's brows knitted as we followed her Dad through the swinging waiter's door leading into the kitchen. The state-of-the-art kitchen had stainless steel appliances, light woods and flat-panel cabinets. Averie's dad shuffled near a bowl sink through a pile of papers. He came back with a solar panel user's manual and a floppy book titled *Photovoltaic Installation*. He rolled them up and shoved them in my bag.

"Give it a shot Big Guy," he punched lightly into my shoulder. "Let me what you figure out anything when you come back to refill the bag."

"Oh," my thoughts snagged on a swirling curiosity, "Yeah. Thanks Mr.?"

"Tom," he said in a husky voice before coughing. "Sorry, I'm just getting over something myself, so I understand how your mom must feel."

"Uh, yeah," I unzipped and then refastened my jacket nervously, "thanks Tom."

Averie and Tom watched as I returned to the snow. I didn't know why, but I refused to look back as I rebounded for the highway. Perhaps I feared that this moment, a time when I navigated through a social encounter unscathed, could shatter if I spotted the simplest grimace or disproving head shake from Averie or Tom. I glanced at the can of fruit cocktail and a small bag of potatoes floating at the top of my bag, and my mouth salivated.

As I crossed the Kelly's blacktop, something else grabbed my attention. There was a baby blue pickup truck parked near the garage that hadn't been there when Averie and I first crossed the highway. The inside was lit up by multiple candles, and I could see three silhouettes huddled together behind the cheap plastic shade. The Kelly's Gas Station was getting fuller, and I hoped that they weren't discussing the two interlopers toying with their generator. I thought about going back to tell Averie, but as I juggled the idea, my sight spun.

There was a tightness in my chest and neck followed by lightheadedness. My anxiety took over as I stammered along the curb that divided the gas station from the highway. I peeled my scarf down and gasped. An invisible blade stabbed between my shoulders, dropping me to a knee. I'd done too much today, and my body was revolting. I don't know how long I sat there, but when I regained my senses, everything was shaking. I needed Mom.

It took all that I had to get to my feet. Every few feet I wobbled, trying to regain my balance like a half-chopped tree. I waddled back home in inches, the once easy to handle grocery bag now weighed as much Atlas's burden. I had hoped someone would notice me and come out to help, but the walk back was silent. With no energy left, I scratched at the door and screamed for Mom. Everything around me faded again as my red nosed Mom opened the door and cried my name. That's when I lost consciousness.

* * *

For days I lay in bed. Mom, not wanting to admit my heart condition could have anything to do with my episode, assured me that my famished state took a toll and that I'd be on my feet in no time. I pretended to agree, but I comprehended the reality. My body had taken a turn for the worst. The first few days were agonizing, but as the pain dulled, so did my entertainment options. We were back to sitting in a cold house with newspaper fires, canned rations and dancing shadows.

Mom kept busy trying to seal a cracked bathroom window that split due to age. She dove into the restroom like a deep-sea diver, bringing cut up insulation from an old attic couch and masking tape for a few minutes at a time before coming back to warm herself by the fire. I was restless, but Mom made me promise to stay in bed. I'd read the books Averie gave me several times over. I'd heard of Holly Black and Neal Shusterman before, but didn't know how much I'd like them. Hearing about fairy wars and fantastical dystopian scenarios made me think the blackout was just a fun plot twist. I wish I had someone to talk to about them.

Going to school went about as well as someone might guess for an ugly kid, and shortly after a week, I'd exiled myself from the world. It was easier to be ugly alone. Following that, Mom homeschooled me while my Dad taught me to be the *man of the house*. What he couldn't show me, I learned in books. I started by fixing the seal on the toilet bowl and later moved on to rewiring the shoddy kitchen electric stove. Anything to keep me busy. Appliances were blind and fixing them made gave me a sense of usefulness. So with Averie on my mind, and a solar panel guide in hand, it was only natural that I tried to see if I could help.

After reading the manuals two or three times, I was confident I could rewire the solar panels. Then Averie and Tom wouldn't need the grid. The only problem was that Mom would not let me leave again. I'd told her about Averie and Tom while I recovered, and while she appreciated their help, she had reservations about me going back, especially because of their proximity to the Kellys. She told me that the Kellys escaped Hell by shooting their way out. They weren't part of the political conflict taking place before the blackout, but they were part of the problem. The Kellys hated anything different from them and were eager to act. Now that there was no one to enforce the law, Mom feared they'd flourish.

Given Mom's passionate disposition, there was only one thing for me to do. I had to sneak out. I didn't like it, but I also couldn't stay in the house any longer, especially if I could fix Averie's electrical problems. I figured I could get out, rewire the panels, and return before Mom ever knew I'd left. So, one late afternoon after Mom left to forage, I dressed in my winter gear again and readied to leave for Averie's house. Before I departed, I took one last picture of my front room in my mind, hopeful but scared that this could be the last time I saw home.

I left to a wet snow beating down on our neighborhood. It tapped on my puffy coat as if to get my attention. I made my way to Pulaski Street, listening to the weather drumming of rooftops. I kept my eyes peeled for abandoned generators near garages and backyards, but as expected, there was nothing. If we wanted a generator, we'd need to figure out how to work with the Kellys.

As I reached Highway 50, I noticed two trucks parked at Kelly's gas station. One, the familiar blue truck, had a bed filled with rusted barrels and canisters. The bed hung low and the overbearing aroma of gasoline stung through my scarf. The other, an orange city truck, kept a steel wedge similar to a locomotive welded to its front. It didn't look like it was being used to shovel the streets. The orange truck kept a gun wrack in the back window and bumper stickers that pledged allegiance to The Faction. In addition, the generator that Averie and I inspected now chained to its chaise. As I squinted through the snow, white light flashed from the station's garage followed by the sounds of hammering. My instincts told me that the Kellys were building something serious inside.

I sat stunned behind a row of bushes along the highway and continued to gawp. Black smoke plumed from the prefabricated metal chimney. A spray of sparks burst from the sausage-shaped garage door glass. It was like watching an angry wasp's nest. I didn't know what was going on, but I realized it was bad. I had to warn Averie and Tom.

I didn't think it would be wise to cross here, so I dissolved back into the landscape of dirty highway homes where I'd come from. I sloshed through the suburbs near the abandoned airport into the prairie hugging Lake Pleasant until I was on the other side of Pulaski Street. The hills and drifts were laboring in my heavy clothing, and as I sweat my way to Averie's yard, my lungs burned as if they were being branded. I ground my teeth as I marched the last few feet to Averie's red door. I clenched my chest while using my free hand to bang on the door. Tom answered, eyes peering from the tops of his glasses.

"Sam," Tom cleared his throat, "are you okay?"

"Yeah, thanks," I gasped. "How about you and Averie?"

"Yes, of course. Why don't you come in."

"Uh, thanks."

I tried to put my hands down to my side, but the torment in my breast wouldn't allow it. Tom didn't seem to notice as he shuffled to the bottom of the stairs and called out for Averie. I took the moment to regain my composure. My body felt like hot food cooling off. Averie shuffled down, smiling until her eyes laid on me. Her beam somersaulted into a long frown. It was nice to have someone other than Mom worried about me as much as it hurt. Averie ran to me, grasping my coat's arm.

"Sam?" she fretted, "Are you okay?"

"Averie," I puffed, "Tom, I'm pretty sure the Kellys know that we were looking at their generator."

"Oh good," Tom retorted, already packing another grocery bag with supplies. "We were trying to figure out how to ask them for it."

"They will not give it to you, Tom," I sat flatly. "They don't share. In fact, they are likely threatened by the idea."

"Sam," Averie rubbed at her arm, biting her bottom lip, "how do you know this?"

I pointed out the door. "I was on my way here when I saw the station. There's two trucks ready for war, filled with gasoline and the generator."

Tom frowned. "Well, Sam that doesn't necessarily mean anything."

"Sam," Averie pulled my arm towards the nearby front room, "Come, sit down." I pulled my arm away, but Averie asserted herself with the puff of her lips. She looked like she was on the verge of angry tears. I gave my arm back to her and let her lead me to a recliner. The front room's fire and my winter clothes worked together to suffocate me, but I refused to remove anything. I struggled to loosen my scarf, lifting it an inch over my mouth to catch a quick breath while keeping my lips concealed. As I did, Averie placed her hand on mine, pulling my scarf down to my neck.

"Sam," she clenched her fingers tightly around my big dumb clawed hand, "I know who you are."

The pain in my chest subsided as anxiety drove my body numb. I was a wild animal caught in a trapper's snare. I sat helplessly on that stupid recliner, too haggard to run, yet too ill equipped to react to what she'd said. *I know who you are.* My neck and shoulders locked. I stared at the dancing fire for quite a while, heaving from my mouth. Averie didn't say a word. Finally, without facing her, and with sweat dribbling down my nose, I spoke.

"How long?" I rasped.

"Like, how long have I known?"

I nodded.

"Oh, I mean, I guessed right away."

"How?"

"Small town."

I pressed my mouth into a hard line, bobbing my head in thought. She'd heard about me before we ever met. I didn't dare look at her. I presumed she was taking in my big chin and bloated lips. It's what everyone did when they saw parts of me. They gawped like you would at a run over squirrel. Only when I finally had the courage to turn to her, she was staring at her gym shoes and wiping tears.

"Uh, why are you crying?" I gibed, "I'm the freak."

"That's exactly why Sam. You're embarrassed."

"Sorry."

"Please don't apologize."

"Oh, uh, sorry."

Averie snorted. "Listen, you don't have to hide Sam. I don't care."

"Uh, no offense Averie, but I'm already super uncomfortable."

"Okay."

"Uh, okay?"

"Yeah, okay. Whenever you think you're ready."

"Oh uh, thanks."

"So," she hesitated, "think the Kellys are coming to get us?"

"Um, maybe, I don't know. I've never met them. Mom told me stories. I wouldn't put it past them."

"And you think they're armed?"

"Even if they're not, they're dangerous, but yeah, likely."

"Any good news?"

"I think I know how to rewire your photovoltaic panels."

"What?"

"Your solar panels."

"Oh, sweet."

My shock wore off and for the first time I focused. My ears heard Tom in the kitchen rearranging cans. He likely had heard none of this. *Thank God*. My chest wasn't heavy any longer. I thought about telling Averie more about me sneaking from my house, my failing body and my worry for Mom, but today had already been too much. *Maybe later.*

"Uh," I put my scarf back over my lower face, "can you ask your dad if he was a wire stripper, pliers and a multimeter?"

"Okay."

"Uh, a wire crimper too, if he can find one."

"Wire stripper, pliers, meter thingy and crimper. Okay I'm totally not going to mess this up."

"I'm just going to take a minute," I pulled the rolled up manual from my inside coat pocket, "double check my work and all that."

Averie squeezed my big shoulder than walked to the kitchen. A storm of angst and uncertainty swirled in my head, but I tried to focus. Fixing things always helped put my mind at ease. I reviewed the manual. I was fairly certain I knew how to prep the panels so they were separate from the grid, given one trouble-making generator. Shortly after, I pushed off the recliner and made my way to Tom and Averie, who were collecting tools inside the connected garage.

"Sam," Tom greeted, holding up a pair of antique pliers, "will this work?"

I nodded. "Uh, yeah. That'll work."

Tom looked over his shoulder to Averie, who shrugged. "I'll get the ladder," he grunted.

Tom and Averie set up the fifteen foot ladder on the side of the house while I stuffed the tools Tom found in my coat pockets. The pair were a good team, working quietly in tandem. When they were done, each of them braced a leg of the ladder as if it reached up to the moon. They watched me as I made it to the first rung. I felt as if rewiring these panels would turn the power back on to the entire world from the way they were looking at me. When I was ready, I nodded to the pair and then clambered my way up through the worsening snow.

"Thanks Sam," Averie lauded before pursing her lips. "You're amazing."

"Sam, should I go up with you?" Tom asked.

"Uh no," I replied over my thoughts. "I don't think there's much you can do up there."

Tom nodded.

I climbed the polished steel rungs of the ladder. My wet boots slipped on the smooth metal as the ladder shook from my weight. I probably looked like Dumbo on the high wire. Tom made time to clean the panels, so the roof was mostly clear to walk. I searched for the main circuit feed under each solar plank. It was hard to ignore the view from up here. The town slept in a frosting kissed with blue as the storms showered down. Smoke from intermittent houses told me that as desolate as the town seemed, we weren't alone.

Once I found the main breaker, it was easy to prep the house. I was meticulous with my repairs and working in the current conditions slowed me down even longer. Nearly an hour later, I'd finished. I threw down the stretched input cable for the generator, and as I did, something caught my ear. It was the rumble of a distant engine. I stiffened my sore back and searched for the source. The gloomy afternoon was handing off its torch to a bleaker night, which made locating the moving headlights from a vehicle even easier.

A pair of trucks drove through the powdery streets towards Tom and Averie's house. I caught the distinct muffled melody of Johnny Cash coming from one cab, even from the handful of blocks between us. My body stiffened. The Kellys were coming, and although I'd thought that'd be the case, I never considered what to do next. My body shook out of its trance and all at once a voice found its way out of my mouth.

"They're coming," I belted as I clambered towards the ladder. "The Kellys are coming." Tom and Averie, who huddled together, looked stunned. I hurried down the ladder, falling down the last six rungs. I stood up with the help of Tom and Averie who were now pulling me to the red door. The pain in my chest returned. Tom snapped the lock behind us. He pressed his back on the red entrance, twisting his lips in thought.

"Sam," Tom peered into my goggled eyes, "no one knows you're here. Go home to your mom. You can use the backdoor." I tried to speak but had lost my breath.

"Dad, wait," Averie disputed. "We can't send him out there alone."

Tom grabbed her by the arms. "Averie, you should go too. Don't worry. I'll take care of this."

"No," Averie pushed him away, "like no way."

I took another strained gulp of air, hoping it would sober me up. Watching the pair quarrel sent my mind parsing. Suddenly, moral economics took rise. I was sure I was dying. Like Mom, Tom and Averie were good people, even in the aftermath of depravity. I couldn't just abandon them. In fact, I *was* the expendable piece in all of this. I understood what I had to do.

"Uh, Averie," I called out. "Where's your back door?" Averie tilted her head, confused. I watched as she worked out what I was asking before shaking back to life.

"Yeah, it's over here," she shook her head. "Come on." Averie didn't second guess me as she made her way to the back of the house. She flipped the locks to the kitchen door before opening it. Frigid winds invaded the warm house, sending loose papers everywhere. Averie gave me one last glance over before nodding and rubbing my arm.

"Uh, thanks for everything Averie," I acknowledged. "It was good to be seen."

"Goodbye Sam," Averie whispered through a weak smile before slowly shutting the door. I listened to her snap the locks. Just then a crash boomed from the front yard.

I hurried passed the grill to the side yard. I cut the corner passed the shed and edged towards the bushes beneath the house's front window. The Kelly's trucks had just rolled through Tom and Averie's yard, smashing into Tom's car. The truck's custom engines rumbled like eighteen-wheelers. Both vehicle doors squealed open as the music turned off. Three silhouettes donned in insulated hunters coveralls stood along the yard. One wore a red Faction hat with ear warmers over it. He studied the house like abstract art while removing a cigar and lighter from his breast pocket. Behind him, a second, short man with a flannel trapper leapt into the bed of the blue truck. He groaned as he lifted a rusted red drum from the vehicle and rolled it out onto Averie and Tom's yard. The third person, a hefty woman with a blue bandana and thick bottle cap spectacles, carried three rifles that she handed out. The man with the cigar puffed at his now lit cigar while checking his rifle.

Adrenaline poured into every muscle, vein and follicle of my body. An implicit ambition called to me from some unknown void. It was primal. I would do whatever it took to protect Averie and Tom. The Kellys, once just unruly town folk, were now my enemies. I leaned into this unfamiliar anger, the only legs of my courage. As the Kellys lined up shoulder-to-shoulder, brashly and confidently staring at the house as if it were feeble prey, a fervor set over me. I hated them all.

The man in the Faction hat whistled as he and the fat woman neared the red door, now with some welded contraption the size of a folding chair in one hand and a rifle in the other. I smelled the sweetness from the man's cigar.

"Yoo-hoo," the cigar smoker called out, his teeth browned from tobacco. He was middle aged, but brawny with silver scruff along his chin. He licked his teeth before continuing. "We have a delivery."

The fat woman, whose face was pink and draped with a dull apricot strand of hair, chuckled. "We understand you need a gas generator?" she jeered while spitting chew. "Come down and sign for it."

The third man, who waited by the truck, opened a gas canister and poured the liquid along the bare parts of the house's walkway. He drew a line down towards the entrance, bumping into the cigar smoking Kelly as he backed along.

"What the hell did I tell you?" the cigar smoking Kelly seethed between the teeth clenching his cigar. "Get that damn gas away from our house."

The Kelly with the gas canister stood up and scratched his head. He had an aquiline nose with a bedraggled mustache and sunken eyes. His skin looked dirty. "Sorry Eustace," the weaselly looking Kelly squeaked, "but I thought you said we wanted to scare em' out."

"I told you to light a fire away from the house," Eustace slapped the weaselly man. "Now get back in the damn truck."

The weaselly Kelly held his cheek while returning to the truck, throwing the now empty canister in the blue truck's bed. The remaining two Kellys left my field of vision as they marched to the front door's stoop. Someone pounded at the door.

"Open up little piggies," Eustace called out, "and let's have a chat." There was a long pause. "Come on, I want to meet that pretty little daughter of yours."

I inhaled a long puff of air through my nostrils, clenched my fists, then skulked along the shores of the front yard towards the truck. The weaselly Kelly now stood in the truck bed, arranging a large drum, as I neared the vehicle's rear. I took one step onto the back bumper and leapt in the truck. My weight shook the vehicle, getting the weaselly Kelly's attention. He froze, his eyes narrowed and jaw slack as I plodded between the cans towards him. Now that I was close enough to sniff his mint gum, I realized how much bigger I was in comparison. He cleared his throat to speak.

My instincts kicked in as my open hands lashed at his neck before he could speak. I took hold and squeezed, the thoughts of Averie being hurt racing in my mind. I put all my weight into it, and as the man silently screamed, we dropped to the bottom of the truck bed. My gloved fingers padded my grip as I lurched over him. *If only my hands were bare, I'd crush his neck.* I didn't know how long I huddled over him, now perched on his chest, but finally the gum rolled out of his cheek and he stopped struggling. I hoped he wasn't dead, but my impulse told me to move on.

"Cody," a female grumbled just outside the truck, "quit playing around and get that gas lit."

I stood up as much as my crooked back would let me. The fat Kelly gasped before lifting her rifle. In the background I saw the smashed red door fractured and ajar. The strange apparatus leaned next to it. The woman fired from the hip as I vaulted towards her. A sharp sting needled in my chest as I pounced on the woman. She groaned as we fell to the lawn, my hands fumbling for the rifle as I winced in pain. I was much stronger than her, and as one hand pressed down on the gun, the other flung my glove off to free my fingers. I rose to my feet; the woman struggling between my legs. I put one boot on her stomach. With a heave I jerked the rifle from her long fake fingernails and turned it on her. She shielded her face, giving me enough time to spin the gun around and club her with the butt of the stock. She didn't go unconscious like in the books, so I hit her again. Her eyes rolled in the back of her head as blood gushed from her temple.

I clambered to my feet and inspected myself. Though the aroma of gunpowder was overwhelming, there wasn't any bullet hole. She'd missed. The agony inside was my heart. My world spun as I strained for breath. My arm numbed and sweat poured from my forehead. I think I was dying. I stumbled to the broken entrance, dropping the gun as I took occasional sideways steps. Before I could make it inside, my knees buckled.

My hand squealed down the frame of glass shouldered along the threshold. My vision narrowed as I retched and gagged. Slowly, I softened to the concrete like melting ice. There was a ringing in my ear from the gunfire. As my breaths became shorter, my body convulsed. I'd failed Tom and Averie.

"Please, no," Averie's scream cut through the house, piercing the noise in my head. I could hear the panic in her voice.

None of the pain went away, but Averie's desperate cries kicked my conscience back in the driver's seat. I told my body to get up. I pushed with my hands and feet until I was upright, leaning on the house for stability. One by one my heavy feet moved forward as I followed Averie's sobbing. I did not understand what I would do when I reached Averie, Tom and Eustace, but it didn't stop me from moving. I shuffled through the front room passed the dining hall and into the kitchen. It took everything I had in me to stay standing under its egress.

Averie and Tom were on their knees, hands behind their heads. Eustace stood behind them and pointed his rifle at their heads. He looked up from the pair at me, his smirk turning into a sneer.

"Get on the ground," he ordered. I took another step. Eustace didn't hesitate. He squeezed the trigger, firing a shot. Averie shrieked. An excruciating sting from my shoulder piled onto the compost pile of aches and pains. Still, I inched forward. Averie's eyes watered. Tom's lip trembled. Eustace cocked his gun. He fired again, driving into my stomach. I tasted copper as the shot took my breath away. Still, I inched forward.

"Damn fool," he jeered as he spit his cigar out. He raised the rifle to his narrowed eye and took aim at my head. I had nothing in me to wince so I just kept shambling along. At least it would be a closed coffin should there ever be a funeral.

But before Eustace fired, Tom bounded from the nylon floor, tackling the Kelly. I limped forward within arm's distance. Eustace was larger than Tom, and spun the dad to the floor, reversing their grapple. Eustace swore as hovered over Tom, who was desperately clawing at the weapon. My naked hand reached out feebly as I pulled at Eustace's hat, dragging it off to reveal a head of long peppered hair. Eustace stared behind him, growling. I scratched at his eyes. Eustace squeezed his eyes shut while continuing to fight with Tom.

Just then, Averie ran to a set of pans hanging over the stove and picked one up. She hurried over to the pile of us. I swear I could hear her skin tighten around the handle. Eustace opened his eyes and took in Averie as she wound the kitchen utensil like a weapon over her head.

"Don't you dare, little girl," Eustace threatened.

Averie pivoted her feet and swung the pan onto Eustace's head. Metal clanked where steel met skull, but Eustace remained upright. Averie must have reached that place because as she raised the pan again, she let out a guttural howl. The skillet met Eustace's temple again, this time driving him into a heap along the kitchen floor. Averie stood over him and screamed. As she did, my weight swayed me backwards, and I joined Eustace on the ground. As anguish and discomfort filled me like fireworks, I noticed that Averie and Tom's ceiling had a leak. *I hope I didn't do that when I was on the roof,* I thought.

My body turned cold and my body numbed. My leg twitched uncontrollably and heard the rubber sole of my boot squealing on the ground. From my peripherals, I made out a pool of red stretch across the fake tile. Perhaps the worse sensation though was the thinning air. I noticed for the first time that I was gasping, my mouth begging for oxygen with each labored breath. I thought I could smell strawberries. Averie's face entered my vision, her wet eyes biting at her eyeliner. She squeezed the scarf now crooked over my nose and mouth.

"No," I gurgled.

Averie's mouth twisted as she took my naked hand. "Sam, I have to. You're dying."

I gulped another painful breath made of jagged glass. "It's not the scarf Averie. It's the bullets and stupid heart."

Averie was taken off guard. She snorted before another tear dripped down her nose and onto my neck. Tom hurried behind Averie to remove fish wire from a drawer and return to Eustace. Averie took her little fingers and pinched the tip of my scarf.

"Please," she pleaded.

"Uh," I coughed uncontrollably. Once my body settled, I added. "Okay."

Averie shaved the scarf from my mouth with a tug. My lips were wet from spittle. She clutched my goggles from my head and squeezed them off my crown before gently placing my head back to the linoleum. I think I'd blamed the goggles for the darkness filtered over my vision, but now that my eyes were free, I realized that wasn't the case. Everything was getting darker. Was that my father, with a proud smile on his face that I had never quite seen before?

I watched what little of Averie's expression I could still see as she took in my entire face for the first time. She must have thought me hideous, a dying monster returning where it belonged. But Averie didn't do that at all. Instead, she stroked my bumpy cheek. I couldn't feel its warmth as she leaned in and kissed me.

"Beautiful," Averie sobbed. "Sam," she cupped her warm hand over my forehead and pet me. "You are beautiful."

PHILADELPHIA

BY PATRICK TILLETT

DAY 690

The old Frenchman sat at a kitchen table, a shallow light from above fixated on a young girl sprawled out on the floor next to him, his voice cut the silence with a rough grit only a smoker had.

"How do you know it's love if you've never been in love before?" she turned her head, looking at him and spoke, trying to sound grown up.

"Cause I feel it." The old man's head tilted to the side in response.

"Where?"

"Right here, in my stomach" she said, holding her belly, which poked out from under her shirt.

The man raised an eyebrow and offered thoughtfully, "Well...that's where your intestines are, maybe it's a shit?"

The actress on the floor snorted out a laugh, then started coughing. The old man acting as the Frenchman sitting in his chair shot up and cursed at the young woman in a very uncouth Philadelphian "Paddy" accent. At this point I had to stifle a laugh from where I was watching off stage left. I didn't do a very good job apparently, because the old man rounded on me with a venomous glare. Before he could get started about the unprofessionalism pervading our theater community, Brian Bannerman, our Director, jumped to my rescue.

"Cliff, just take a beat, alright? There's no reason for that kind of language, and don't abuse your costars." Cliff decided it was the director's turn to catch his daggers, but turned and stormed off without further outburst, announcing to the entire Walnut Street Theater he would be in his dressing room. Janet, the young woman who had been opposite of Cliff, stood up and apologized to Brian.

"I'm sorry, I know you say it's not a big deal but-" she was interrupted when Brian waved her words away.

"And it really isn't. I know you're a little younger than a lot of us, so you probably don't remember before the lights went out." Cliff Carlyle was a prominent stage actor before the electricity had cut off across the country, and he had shown up in a couple of popular TV Shows and movies back then too. Brian explained he was one of those guest actors who got called in to fill a role, like William Shatner before Star Trek (Janet didn't understand that one, I don't know what I expected), but he never quite made it. Maybe he always figured there would be time to break out, but then the world stopped turning one day, and theater was all he had left.

I heard there was a little more to it than that. Cliff was something of a local celebrity in Philly in those days, with all that entailed, including the messy divorce. As the story goes, Cliff's kids were staying with their mother when everything went down. Apparently, he used to go out for days on end to look for his kids and their mom in the city. Back then, when the world was first changing, you didn't know what to expect. No one did. Nobody ever asked him why, but one day he just stopped going. So maybe I understand why he gets so ornery when it comes to his craft.

"Just because Cliff needs some cool down time in his dressing room doesn't mean rehearsal is shot. Janet, you take your spot for scene three for me. Michael! I need you onstage!" Brian continued shouting instructions, telling people where to stand. It was like watching a kid set up his toys before an extravagant imaginary battle. I jogged out to my starting place too, just another one of the toys. Cliff came back out after about half an hour, gave an apology, and the rest of our rehearsal for Besson's "Leon, The Professional" went off without a hitch.

Afterwards we went to the Oarhouse, a tavern near the theater, to unwind as a group. No matter how much things got twisted out of shape, some food and drink set them right for us. I think that's true for most things, actually, but that's not why it was important that we went out for drinks. It's important because that was where I met Douglas Lorie for the first time.

I didn't quite notice him at first, he looked like he was in his early twenties, not quite able to grow facial hair yet, with dark hair a few inches long. Maybe if I had come in looking for someone, he would have struck me immediately, but that night I was on a mission with my friends.

We were chatting and drinking the cool beer that Pete served us from behind the bar for quite some time. They brewed it down in the basement, where a natural root cellar was built to keep it cooler than the main bar upstairs. Of course it was never ice cold, but what are you gonna do? I wasn't sure what time it was when Cliff, the last of us other than myself, decided to call it a night. I watched the man pull on his old coat as he shuffled to the door, bracing for the wind that rarely gave up cutting through the corridors made by the city's buildings, which had been predominantly abandoned in the last few years.

As the door clicked shut behind Cliff, my attention turned to the rest of the bar's meager patronage. That was when I really took a good look at Douglas and wished I had done it sooner. I ordered two more from Pete and made my way over to his table, sitting down in a chair opposite him.

"Is it alright if I sit here? It's awfully crowded tonight." I waved one of my glasses around the empty tavern while I slid the second towards him. "I got you something to pay my table rent." Douglas smiled with a quiet exhale from his nose, but he took my drink graciously.

"Good thing you did too, Lord knows I'd hate to turn you away. Name's Douglas, Douglas Lorie. Yourself?" He sipped his beer while introducing himself.

"Michael Ford, and it's a pleasure to meet you Douglas. Are you from the city? I haven't seen you in here before."

"Are you here every day, that you recognize every patron of the Oarhouse? I gotta say, if you're flirting right now, implying you have a drinking problem is an interesting strategy." He laughed at me, a high lilting thing that went straight to your head in a funny way. It was a good laugh.

"I'm only here often enough to know all the charming, good looking men, and I don't know you. Yet." I was still sipping and leaned forward on one arm. "Does it feel like I'm flirting?" We shared a momentary silence, but a comfortable one.

"So how often do you and your friends come by?"

"Only after rehearsals, it's sort of a ritual."

"Rehearsal?" He cocked an eyebrow. "Tell more."

"Well..." I laughed sheepishly. "I'm an actor. We all are, we perform at Walnut Street up the road a bit."

"An actor? Now that's something I never thought I'd hear. Do people still see shows after the Outage?" He stopped to think for a second. "And what do you guys do? You can't be using film, there's no power to display it, unless..." he lowered his voice as if to keep Pete (the only other person in the bar) from hearing. "Do you guys have power? Like a generator or something?"

I couldn't help but laugh out loud, which got Pete's attention. Lucky, actually, because we were out of drinks.

"No, no, we don't have power, or film, or even cameras. We do perform famous films though, only we do them on stage instead. And putting aside my holier-than-thou indignation: Yes, Douglas, people do still come to see shows. See, people are always going to need entertainment, a distraction to keep us sane. My job is to keep great stories alive in our memory."

"I take it back then, you're a regular Homer." He paused and unsubtly looked me up and down. "With much better cheekbones."

"So you know why I'm here, although I don't appreciate being called an alcoholic…" Douglas winked at me over his glass. "But you haven't answered my question. What brings you here tonight?"

"I'm looking for someone." he smirked. "You could say I'm visiting family."

"Well which is it? Looking for someone or visiting family?" I asked, and he only answered me by sipping his drink silently. "Looking for family?" I guessed. He smiled and I knew I hit the nail on the head. "Okay stranger, now it's your turn to tell more."

"How much time have you got?"

"For this? I've got all night." I leaned the chair back on its hind legs and got comfortable.

So Douglas told me about his village outside of Philadelphia; a small collection of cabins that rested in the woods past the Benjamin Franklin bridge. They were nestled on the far side of the river and lived predominantly off the land, growing food while several of their community went out to hunt the wildlife that shared their home. By all counts it was idyllic, albeit rustic. Douglas himself lived with his mother, helping her harvest the crops. He explained that he got sick often and wasn't any good for hunting as a result. The problem was, his mom did too, and one day, she got sick and couldn't kick it.

"Jesus, I'm sorry…" I said, feeling like an ass. "What was it? Wasn't there anyone who could help? Your dad maybe?" Douglas laughed a mirthless chuckle.

"One would think, right? She never said much about him, but Dad was never in the picture for me. Some of the older folks in the village told me he was someone important who used to make the trip over the bridge to see her, but I guess raising a kid after the power loss was something he thought was too much trouble." Douglas drained the last of his drink. "After mom went, I decided I was gonna come here and find my old man myself."

"What happens then? And how are you gonna find him?" I asked.

"Don't know yet, but I do have one lead on how to get to him." he gave me a meaningful look.

"What, me?" I asked, incredulous.

"According to everyone who could tell me about him, he was some big shot back in the day, so I figure he's probably part of the upper class here, right?" Douglas spoke energetically with his hands. It was true there was some manner of aristocracy in the city, mostly well-off folks who donated their space, clothes, or shelter to create the community here in Philly. They were considered good people here, though, and I could hardly believe one of them leaving anyone, let alone their flesh and blood, in such an awful position. "The fat cats, don't they come to your theater to see you guys perform?"

"I suppose…"

"Is there any way that you can get me onto your stage? It's the best shot I have at finding him." he looked at me now, playful flirting gone, all emotion and pleading.

"I mean, maybe." I shook my head to clear my thoughts. "But look, this is my life, okay? If I stick my neck out for you like this, I need your word that you won't cause trouble. Can you promise me that?"

"Ford, I promise I'm not here to ruin your show. I'm just a person looking for someone who owes them a debt." If that ain't the truth, I thought.

"I don't suppose you have any place to stay tonight, do you?" Douglas shook his head and I sighed. "Then I guess you're staying with me, and we can talk to Brian in the morning."

"Yes! Thank you so much! Where do you live?" he asked.

"I'll give you three guesses, and the first two don't count." We went home after I settled my tab with Pete, and returned to my apartment, a repurposed dressing room in the Walnut Street Theater.

I woke up the next morning with the sun shining rudely in my eyes through naked blinds. I had fallen asleep on the couch while I offered the simple twin bed up to Douglas, who graciously accepted. Sometimes it can hurt to be such a good host, as I was quickly learning. Luckily Douglas was a light sleeper and was already awake with hot coffee waiting for me, which I took with an appreciative grunt as thanks.

"Ah, I see you're one of those people." he laughed at my expense. He seemed more chipper than he did the previous night.

"You seem like you're in a better mood, too early to curse your tragic life?" I grumbled, forcing my eyes open as I turned my back to the sun.

"No that doesn't usually happen till dark." he quipped. "But I can't be grim and moody all the time. Besides, we have to talk to your friend, right? The sooner, the better."

He was right, and after two quick wash ups in my basin, we were downstairs just in time to see Brian arriving for his "rituals", as he called them. He always came by in the late morning, a few hours before the others, to quality check anything he could think of and then make necessary repairs. Usually I was a late sleeper, so he was understandably surprised to see me waiting on stage for him with my coffee, and doubly surprised to see we had company.

"Who's this, Michael? You don't usually bring strays around here." Brian asked, gesturing to Douglas sitting by me.

"This is Douglas, we got to talking at the Oarhouse after you guys left last night, and he wanted to ask you about working with us." I explained.

"Well that's too bad, I have enough actors already."

"I'm actually not an actor, so that wouldn't be an issue." Douglas spoke for himself. "I write, I can put together plays and help you with the stage work."

"Yeah, but I already got a show, too." Brian said, but he rubbed at his chin thoughtfully. "I can always use good hands though...You said you can do set work? Have any experience?"

Douglas shrugged in response. "Not on the stage, as such, but I grew up on farmland, so I know how to work with my hands. Besides, I can stick around long enough for you to show me anything you need taken care of."

"What about it, Brian?" I asked. "Not a bad deal, right? How many times have we been begging for volunteers during Hell Week?"

"Yeah, you got a fair point there." Brian grumbled and mumbled to himself for a minute, before sizing Douglas up with a long, hard stare. "You got a place to stay?" Brian looked at Douglas, and Douglas looked at me. I looked at Brian.

"He does, I'm sleeping on the couch for the time being." I answered.

"Huh. So what about you, Ford, do you need a place to stay?" He asked me, laughing at himself. Douglas laughed too, but little did they both know, I seriously considered it for a second before laughing along with the both of them. That was how Douglas came to be a regular member of the theater with us.

Show night was still several weeks away, so there was plenty of time for all of us to get acclimated. Douglas was learning about running the behind-the-scenes minutiae of the stage, and we all learned how to work with him. He hadn't lied to Brian; he was good with his hands. He could maintain and repair anything we needed, provided we gave him the tools and materials to handle the job. It was the technical aspect of theater that he needed help in. He missed cues for some time because he just didn't know the terminology. Cliff joked that maybe if we made all the ropes different colors, we could train him like a rat. That hadn't remained a problem for long, because Douglas was a relentless study. I stayed up long nights teaching him about the job, often sneaking down to the stage, literally showing him the ropes until he became proficient. After two weeks of these regular lessons, he was like a fish tossed back in the water -- a natural. To be honest I didn't mind staying up with him even after he didn't need our lessons anymore, and I don't think he did either.

I asked him one day what his plan was after finding his father. Would he stay here, or was he going to disappear back into the wide world he came from? He was unsure, to say the least.

"It's not like I haven't thought about it." he sat with his bare back against the window, cooled by late night Atlantic rains. "I can see this plan, how I'll find him, so clearly." Douglas closed his eyes. "I can see the theater, full of people. And I'm looking, looking from backstage. I know he's out there."

"How will you know it's him?" I asked. The candle lights of our room cast half his face in shadow, like a dramatic painting.

"I'll know it's him." he simply answered. "For anything else, he's my dad. He'll look like me, and after the show I'll find him in the lobby and then…" Douglas' brow furrowed. "But when I imagine what comes next: What I'll say and do after I meet him…I don't see anything. So I don't really know what happens next." He opened his eyes, which were darkened by the dim light. He blew out an exasperated sigh and pushed his hair back. "I guess I'll just give him a piece of my mind and go from there."

"Great things were built from lesser plans, I guess." I rolled over on my makeshift futon, looking up at the rafters while I thought to myself. What did I want to hear? And why was I so invested in this? Granted, it was all terribly romantic, but what was I doing? Douglas was gorgeous, that went without saying, but I had met handsome men before and I never invited them into my home while searching for their mysterious lost family.

"You're being awfully quiet now, what's on your mind?" Douglas asked. I rolled my eyes up from the ceiling to see him on the bed now. From my perspective, the whole world was upside down. His world probably seemed that way too.

"I'm thinking dress rehearsal is tomorrow, and opening night after that." I realigned myself to earth's gravity. That is to say, I rolled over onto my stomach. "We should go to sleep."

The final rehearsal the next day went as smoothly as it could. We were each allowed to have one breakdown, Brian said at the beginning, although they couldn't be longer than five minutes each. We started earlier than normal, nearly as the sun was rising, and didn't stop until the sun was gone and the candles low. Douglas was sent outside all day to put up more advertisements and drum up last minute interest in our production. As with every other job he had been given, he jumped at the opportunity. He said it was just a better chance to put eyes out, and maybe he would be lucky enough to bump into the guy he was looking for. It was late that night, or early the next morning perhaps, when he came back to the apartment and he didn't look as though his day had been fruitful.

"Any luck?" I asked, although I wasn't confident. Douglas tossed a few unused pamphlets onto a table I kept in the middle of the room.

"Not so much, it would seem." He said with a beleaguered sigh. The glint in his eyes gave a hint of sly optimism, however. "I had an idea, though."

"Oh?" I knew him well enough so far to know he would share, even without my asking.

"So you know Hamlet, right?" he asked.

"Not personally, no."

"Very funny. But specifically, do you remember the part in Hamlet where he puts on a play to test his uncle's guilt?"

"Who put on a play?" I was toying with him.

"Hamlet did… Wait, have you not read Hamlet before?" Douglas asked, unsure if I was just screwing with him. I rolled my eyes with a smile. I had to keep him on his toes, after all. "Of course you have, you dick."

"I never claimed to be otherwise, but more importantly:" I rolled my hand in a circular motion to let him know that I was listening. "Go."

"Right, the plan." Douglas cleared his throat. "In Hamlet, he...you know, Hamlet, put on a play about a King's brother who killed the King and stole his wife and crown, all so he could watch his uncle in the audience and judge his guilt. I want to do the same thing to find my dad!"

"We're already doing a play though." I said.

"I know, but we can add a scene. Just one." He held up one finger to emphasize his point. "One where Mathilda confronts her father, or his ghost maybe, for being so evil and abandoning them." I cocked an eyebrow, because Mathilda's dad didn't abandon his family in the show. "Neglect is a form of abandonment, don't look at me like that."

"Fine, so we write this little extra scene in. Then what?"

"I will be waiting in the wings, observing the audience. And when our own Claudius starts to fidget and get uncomfortable, then I'll confront him in person." He looked at me expectantly. "Well? How about it?"

"You want to know what I think?" I asked, and he nodded vigorously. "It all sounds very...Shakespearian."

"In a good way, like it's well thought out?" Douglas suggested.

"The opposite actually. Like there's about a million ways it could go wrong." Douglas hung his head, dejected. "But you and I... You've been working on this for way too long to not try every last trick you can think of. I'll get everyone together early tomorrow morning, and we'll talk it over. They all need to know what's happening if we're going to try your plan."

Douglas was giddy, but it was late and suddenly we had another early morning ahead of us. Despite his rush of energy, we both settled down for bed. I didn't know it at the time, but that would be Douglas Lorie's last night in Philadelphia. Early the next morning, well before Brian typically came in for his routine, we had assembled the entire cast at the theater. They were about as receptive of the idea as I thought they would be.

"Absolutely not!" Brian protested loudly. "There is no way in hell that we are going to make changes to the production this late! It's opening night for Christ's sake!"

"It is extremely short notice, Michael." chimed in Janet. "I mean, maybe if we had time to rehearse it, but twelve hours before curtain? It's impossible."

"I know you think that, but..." Douglas was interrupted again by Brian, who had exploded at the idea of making changes to his script.

"NO, NOT EVEN IF WE HAD MORE TIME!" There was a vein in Brian's forehead that was pulsing at an alarming rate, and his face was beet red as he rounded on Douglas. "And YOU! When I let you in with us, you didn't even know how to tie down a curtain! I trusted you, and here you are trying to steal my play from me!" Douglas balked in offense.

"Steal your play? Mr. Bannerman, this isn't about you! I don't want to ruin your play, I..."

"You don't want to ruin it? So this is about being able to do it better than me?" Douglas seemed to be on the verge of tears in his frustration, but I was starting to get pissed off. How dare Brian talk down to him like that? All this time, I thought we were a damn team, but he was tearing this kid down like a drill instructor having a bad day.

"You and I have worked together for a long time, Brian, but this is the first time I've ever seen you act like a spoiled child!" I jumped into the fray. "For the last time, this isn't about you, Douglas is just trying to find his dad and I want to help him! So maybe you could put away your pride for three minutes and have a mature conversation with us!"

"Alright, that's enough Michael. Brian, calm down and listen." Cliff interjected. He had been quietly sitting down thus far, listening. Apparently, he had heard enough and was ready to put in his two cents. "I don't know why you feel so threatened by the kid, but you clearly do."

"What? I-I'm not-" Brian stammered, still red in the face. Cliff put up both hands and closed his eyes pensively.

"Maybe you aren't. Maybe you're just having a bad day, lord knows it's a tough situation. But you're a damn fine director. Damn fine. It's gonna take more than one scene added to a classic film to derail that talent." Brian's forehead vein slowed, as did his hyperventilation. "Look at these kids, it's clearly important to Douglas and Michael, and art is constantly evolving anyway. I say we can get it done." He shrugged and said those were just his thoughts.

As he left, the rest of us turned toward Brian, since we weren't going to be able to pull this off without his support. He looked us all in the eyes, thinking for a tense moment of silence. At last, his shoulders dropped, and he blew a long breath out through his nose.

"Alright, we'll try this addition..." Brian sighed, and he raised one finger, leaning towards Douglas before walking off. "But you only get ONE scene. The rest of the show goes on as rehearsed."

While Douglas sat down with Brian to hammer out the dialogue for his plan, I went outside to find Cliff sitting on a bench across the road, smoking a hand rolled cigarette.

"Mind if I take a seat here?" I asked him.

"Do whatever, Mike, I'm not your dad." he answered softly without looking at me.

"Funny choice of words." I laughed through my nose and sat down next to my older colleague. From this seat you could see in through the open windows of the theater. Skylights in the roof let in more light, illuminating the stage. I could see Douglas directing people on stage, with Brian standing behind him telling them where to go instead. Cliff must have been watching them just like I was. "Why'd you convince Brian for us?"

"What's that?" he asked.

"I appreciate the assist and all, but it seemed out of character for you to stick your neck out like that for me and Douglas." I explained.

"It was more for the kid, actually." Cliff wasn't smoking anymore. His cigarette just burned absently in his fingers, the only thing it was capable of. "You said he was looking for his old man back there. That's probably the only reason he ever came to this place." Cliff looked up and down the street, lined on both sides by buildings with greenery creeping up the facade. Each one was an echo of what it once had been, even if they were repurposed. Each one was changed. Cliff kept talking, but I felt that he had forgotten I was there. "I spent a long time looking for my family. Never found 'em. Now this theater is all I got. It's a good theater, but…"

"I get it." I said, standing up. I clapped Cliff on the shoulder and gave him an understanding smile. "It's a good theater, but it doesn't have to be all he has."

"Doesn't have to be all you have either, Mike. Get in there, tell Brian I'll be back in a few." Cliff lifted what was left of the cig to his lips, renewing the flame as he sucked air through it. The door to the theater was thrown open and Douglas was hanging on the handle.

"Can you two get in here, already? Brian thinks we should use Cliff to play her father, since Leon is a father figure in the script anyway!!" he shouted.

"Don't give away the whole plot, what if someone outside hasn't seen it before?" I called back, crossing the road. Douglas grinned sheepishly, buzzing with energy again. We all tried to match that energy while we worked on this last scene before opening.

* * *

"Douglas, heads up! Your scene is up next, they're setting the stage now." I warned Douglas backstage in a hushed whisper.

"I think I'm gonna be sick." He muttered back. He looked like it too. His face was utterly pale and stood in stark contrast to the dark hair. "I don't know if this is gonna work, there's so many people out there!"

"It's okay, keep your voice down. Now look at me." I clasped his hands in mine while I looked deep in his eyes. His eyes were a gorgeous brown, a deep hue like rich earth when it's lit up by a sunrise; the kind of earth that you know has untold treasures and gems hidden just beneath the surface. How had I not paid attention to his eyes before? "This is what you've been waiting for. Everything's set, so we're gonna do the scene. I'll take over here so all you need to do is hide and watch the audience. This is going to work, Douglas Lorie."

"And if it doesn't?" It felt like he was searching for answers in my own eyes. My palms felt warm against his clammy hands.

"Then I'll be here." I let him go and took over his position. I mouthed at him to go on, and good luck. Silently, he whispered a quick thank you before dashing off. I pulled the curtains open.

The stage was set in disarray. Janet entered from stage-left and anxiously made her way toward center. She was surrounded by the debris of destroyed furniture and fake blood was smeared on the walls. It was Mathilda's old apartment, still in ruins long after her family had been murdered by corrupt police. Cliff sat waiting in one of the only intact chairs.

"What are you doing here?" asked Janet meekly, channeling the emotional uncertainty of her character, Mathilda.

"I'm waiting for you to come home." answered Cliff, simultaneously playing Leon and Mathilda's father. It was a bit avant-garde. "Isn't that what Daddies are supposed to do?"

"What Daddies are supposed to do?" she mimicked, audibly upset. Janet let out an incredulous laugh. "How the hell are you supposed to know what Daddies do for their daughters?"

Her father/Leon/Cliff remained silent in the chair, looking up at the actress yet still down the bridge of his nose.

"You're supposed to have a job! To keep us safe!" Janet let her voice betray more emotion, cracking with tears hiding behind her eyes. "You're supposed to be at home, waiting for your kids to come home from fucking school! The world outside is evil, and violent, and parents are the ones who teach us how to make it better!" Janet was acting with her full body now, her arms gesturing broadly with every line, and tears streaming from her eyes. By now, she was completely Mathilda, confronting someone she should have been able to depend on who betrayed her. "You abandoned us to the world, you old bastard. What do you have to say for yourself?"

"I don't have anything to say." Cliff said simply. "I was never there, and I'm not here now."

On cue, I drew a shade over the skylights in the ceiling to cast the stage in shadow. Less than a minute later, when I had drawn the shade back again, Cliff was gone, and Janet was standing alone in the wreckage. From where I was standing, I saw a man leaving and Douglas was following a short distance behind him. I cursed to myself, looking around. Onstage, Janet was reciting her monologue and there weren't any stagehands around to take over for me. A pair of older, calloused hands wrested control of the rope from me, and Brian tapped me on the shoulder.

"Go on, I'll take over here." He whispered, nodding his head toward the exit. I nodded my thanks and dashed out the back door and through a hallway that spat me out at the lobby. Out here, the scene was even more dramatic than the display inside.

Douglas was face to face with the man who had left during his scene. The stranger was standing with his arms crossed over his chest. He was dressed in a suit jacket over a buttoned shirt and jeans. The jacket was loose fitting and looked like it was tailormade so that it would be more durable. While Douglas was holding a hostile stance, this man looked considerably angrier at being stopped.

"I don't know who the hell you are, kid, but you can back off right now and go back to your stupid play with the rest of your hack friends." He said in a crass voice.

"I'm not going anywhere until you admit it, you left because the scene in there made you uncomfortable. And you're uncomfortable, because you're GUILTY, because you left us behind!" Douglas shouted, poking this man in his chest.

"I told you, you're not my son you little runt! I don't have any damn kids, and if I did and they turned out like you?" he scoffed. "Well, I can understand why your daddy left you behind with some bitch."

He probably thought he had gotten the last word in, but before I could step in to defuse the situation Douglas leaped on top of the guy and was slugging him in the face with both hands. I dashed out as fast as I could to pull him off.

"Douglas, calm down! I think it's safe to say you've got the wrong guy!" Douglas' breathing calmed slightly, and I let him go so I could help the older man off his back. He was less than appreciative.

"Get your damn hands off me." He pushed me away and pointed at the both of us, blood trailing from his nose and mouth. "I may not know who the hell THIS little rat is, but I at least recognize you, Ford. If this is how your friends treat customers, then I promise you won't have another show in this town again!" He pushed his hair out of his face and stormed out the door, pausing in the open door frame. "And for the record: I left because that scene SUCKED. If you're going to shoehorn in additions to classic performances, at least make sure it isn't sophomoric garbage!"

He slammed the door shut and left us alone in the lobby. I was panting, and Douglas was still seething with rage. I turned to him and without a word, he stormed upstairs to the apartment. I wanted to follow him, but I knew the show was still running and I couldn't stay out here forever.

"What am I doing here?" I muttered to myself, taking the stairs up two at a time. At the door to my apartment, I heard shuffling and muffled muttering. Opening the door, I found Douglas cramming clothes into his rucksack.

"What happened down there?" I asked calmly, closing the door behind me. He stopped pacing and packing but kept his head down and wouldn't meet my eyes.

"Go back downstairs and finish your show." his voice croaked and trembled.

"Douglas, I'm not going to leave you like this." I crossed the room to him, but he turned his back to me and looked out through the window. "Talk to me." There was a long silence, until at last he spoke again.

"I knew it wasn't him." Douglas said in a flat, deadened voice. "Once I saw him in the light...he didn't even look like me. I just..." he leaned his forehead against the window. "I just wanted to hold somebody accountable."

"Accountable for what? I know your dad left you and your mom, Douglas, but it was years ago, wasn't it?"

"I don't care about any of that, we did fine without him. But she's dead, Ford." At last, Douglas turned around to face me. He was all red cheeks and bloodshot, puffy eyes. He had been sobbing in here, and probably had been from the moment he was alone in the stairwell. "My mother is dead, and I'm the only one left who cares. I came all the way to Philly to find my dad, and now I'm still here, alone!"

"What was finding your dad supposed to accomplish?" I asked him.

"I don't know, alright? Even if I had found the old man, if he's even still alive, then I don't know what it would mean for me." he was flustered, looking all over, flailing his arms while he talked. He also took up pacing again.

"Was it ever about your dad?" he didn't respond, he just sat there in defeated silence. "I think you just ran away, and I get it Douglas. Really, I do."

"No you don't. I was out working when it...I never even got to say goodbye."

"No, I do understand. I lost my mom before the Power Loss, man. Picture that. We lived in a world with power, cars, fuel, comfort, and medicine. We had every conceivable advantage, and she still passed away. I remember I was on the way to the hospital to see her when I got the call." My cheeks grew a little hotter as I recounted the story. "I trusted that she would be alright in a hospital at least long enough for me to see her, but when I stopped for gas, I got a phone call from my dad. He just said not to come. That she was gone, and I should just turn around and go back home. Like she had just stepped out somewhere and I missed her."

"Why are you telling me this?" Douglas asked me. He was sitting on the edge of the bed now, head in his hands.

"I'm telling you this because I know you'll understand. We've felt the same loss, and Douglas, as much as it hurts..." I knelt down in front of him and took his hands again, like before in the theater. "As much as it hurts, finding some asshole who left you two behind won't bring her back."

"What then?" His lip started to tremble again. "What do I have, besides a bunch of memories that I can't decide if I'm better off keeping because they hurt so damn much?"

"You have those memories, and trust me, you will want to hold them as close as you can." I took a chance, looking into those big brown eyes. I leaned up and kissed him on the corner of his mouth, just a peck. "And you have me. I told you earlier that I'd be right here. Well here I am, if you'll have me." Our gazes locked and electrically charged moments passed between us, punctuated only by our heartbeats.

"Michael Ford..." Douglas pulled me up off the floor into a tight embrace, and I held him back. Our hug turned into kisses, small ones at first but they rapidly grew deeper, more passionate. I climbed into bed on top of him and he reached up to undo my shirt. I broke away from him just long enough to look at him one more time.

"Is this okay?" I asked, breathless.

"Shut up." He pulled me back against him and the sun set below the horizon and the skyline outside while we enjoyed each other at last. Hours had passed before there was a knock at my door, interrupting us from the contented silence that followed.

Standing up, I pulled some pants on and went to the door to find Brian outside. I had completely forgotten about the show.

"Oh my god, Brian, I'm so sorry! I have no-" he held a hand up against my apologies and excuses.

"It's fine, Michael, it's already done. The show went off without a hitch…" He eyed Douglas, who was still in bed under a cover. "Or should I say, nearly without a hitch. Can I come in?"

"Um, sure." I opened the door the rest of the way and waved him inside. "So, I think I might know what you're referring to."

"Oh, I hope so." Brian nodded sarcastically. "The guy who left early tonight…" He pointed at Douglas, who was trying to get dressed inconspicuously. "The one you assaulted, that is -- just happens to be something of an influence in this town. We found him down at the Oarhouse while we were looking for you two. Needless to say, he's pretty pissed."

"Oh god…" Douglas moaned. "I am so sorry, what can I do?"

"Nothing to be done, he wanted the theater shut down for good." Brian said definitively. "However after no small amount of brownnosing, not to mention the amount of money I had to spend to pay off his tab, he agreed to leave us be."

"Well that's a relief." I said, "I swear, Brian, this is never going to happen again."

"I know." Brian answered gravely, "Because the pompous ass had one more condition. You and Douglas have to leave town. Tonight."

"What?" I had to have misheard him.

"You heard me right the first time. The guy says he's coming back tomorrow morning, and if either of you two are still here or anywhere else in town, he'll know about it. And he said he'll organize the folk here to shut us down for good."

Brian explained. "Like I said, it's already done so there's no point in me getting angry. I just can't ask all the others to pack up and head out into the wilderness."

That was all he had to say. The three of us sat in silence and I looked at Douglas again.

"Ford, I'm so sorry…" He started to say.

"No, don't be. Brian, we'll be out of your hair before sun-up. And there's no hard feelings, really." I told him. Brian didn't say anything back, but he pulled me into a big hug to say goodbye. We clapped each other on the back, and he left me to pack up whatever I needed.

"What are you gonna do?" Douglas asked after he had gone.

"What am I gonna do? I was hoping we'd be in this together, ya know, after tonight." Douglas cracked a smile and gave a wry laugh, then we shared a quick kiss.

"Alright, together then. I was gonna go back home and visit my mom's resting place. I don't suppose you'd be interested in joining me?" he asked, helping me pack up.

"I'd be honored to join you, and you can tell me about her on the way."

"It's a long trip back, even after getting over the bridge." he responded.

"Then it's good that we've got a lot to talk about."

"Michael?"

"Yeah?" I answered him. I liked when he called me Michael.

"Thank you."

True to our word, we left while it was still dark out. There were torches and lamps that lit the streets at night, but as we left the town streets behind and homes became more sparse, so did the lights to guide us. We had just made it onto the Benjamin Franklin bridge out of Philadelphia when we decided to rest and wait until sunrise to go further. It was dangerous to be fumbling around in the dark on the old thing anyway, that high up over cold waters. We spent the entire time talking, sharing stories. Douglas told me a lot about growing up with his mother. She was warm and caring, funny, and above all, kind. I told him she reminded me a lot of my mom, and that I would have loved to meet her sooner.

"Thanks, that means a lot." Douglas said, we were taking our break inside a toll booth at the base of the bridge. It was cramped, but I didn't mind sharing it with him. "I'm content for us to get to know each other now."

"I'll be around as long as you want me, Douglas." I said as the night sky very gradually began to lighten.

"Forever, then?" He asked. He looked at me and his brown eyes were glowing with the promise of a new day, reflecting the newly rising sun. I felt my heart skip a beat at the thought of life with Douglas Lorie. I grinned.

"Forever, then."

MY CONSTANT FRIENDS THE STARS

BY SILENCIO MARQUEZ

DAY 2.938

When I was eight years old, the world changed. It was the year the lights went out, the year my mother was in a terrible car accident, and the year she died. In fact, it was the lights going out that caused her death. Which was why I was where I am now -- An orphan working as a farmhand in Eastern Oregon.

I laid out in the field on the crisp summer grass and gazed up at the stars. Through everything, they'd been my constant companion. They glimmered brightly above me in an endless sea of darkness. They would be there even long after I and everyone I knew was gone. I didn't know why they were bringing back these memories tonight. I didn't want to think about those kinds of things. They reminded me I was an orphan now.

I heard the grass crunching under someone's feet nearby. "Kyle, is that you?" I hoped it was him, but I really didn't want to get up. It'd been a long day and I was tired. These fields hadn't planted and harvested themselves.

"I knew you would be here," I heard him say as he came and sat down next to me. "You're so damn predictable."

"Did you want something?" I could only see so much of him in the darkness. Just a mop of dark hair. If it were light, I'd be able to see his emerald green eyes. But all that was lost in the darkness. I could only make out what the dim moonlight allowed me to see.

"Not really. I just wanted to talk to someone other than my mom. She's bugging me again about going to the city and becoming something other than a farmer."

"That's a terrible idea," I said. "I came out here to be a farmer, or at least to work on a farm. The city is dangerous these days. Not even the suburbs are safe. I mean, my father was shot in the street in broad daylight."

He laid down next to me. "That's what I told her, Jace. I'm beginning to think she's not very smart."

"Be nice. She's your mom."

"I know. She's just trying to look out for me."

"At least you have parents who can look out for you."

Kyle gave a long sigh. "You keep reminding me you're a sad orphan."

I turned over onto my side, glaring into the side of his head. "You're a dick sometimes."

"I know. So, what's going on in the heavens tonight?"

I laid back, again, looking into the starry depths of the Milky Way. "Everything. Away from the oil lamps of the city, you can see everything. I think this is the way it was always supposed to be."

"When was it not like this?"

"When there were lights. Your dad told me. It used to be in the city you couldn't see any of this. There were too many lights."

I felt his hand touch mine. I couldn't help but take his hand in mine and hold it tight. "Are you ever going to tell your parents about this?"

"That I love you? I think they already know. You live here. Do you think they're blind?"

"You're the one who said your mom wasn't very smart."

"Trust me, she picked up on it."

"Is she okay with it? Her son being together with an orphan from the city?"

"I don't think she cares. I don't think either of them cares."

"Do you think they'd care if we got married?"

There was a pause. I'd thought about asking him in the past, but the time was never right. Had he never thought about it?

"I never knew you were that serious about it."

"What?" I was baffled. I'd been working on his parent's farm for two years since leaving the city after my father's murder. Kyle and I had hit it off almost immediately, spending time together watching the stars on several occasions. We'd even made love in this field. I couldn't believe that he didn't think that we were serious. "Are you fucking kidding me?"

"Sure, we live in the same house, we've spent a lot of time together, we've fucked, but that doesn't mean that I want to spend the rest of my life with you."

"Why not?"

"Because I don't love you."

He was being honest. I could hear it in his voice. He'd been fine when we were just casual lovers, but now reality was hitting him, and he didn't like it. I took my hand back from him. "You don't love me? Fine, then I guess we're done. I'll be leaving in the morning."

"Back to the city?"

"Fuck no. There's still no damn law and order there. I'll find another farm to work on or something."

"Or something?"

"Something is better than nothing, which is apparently what I have with you."

"Suit yourself." I could hear the annoyance in his voice. He was angry with me. He had no right to be. He got up and left me alone there in the field. I tried desperately not to cry. I'd cried too much in the last four years. Whatever this was, it was over, and I had to move on. I found Orion in the sky above me. It would be fall soon. This was the worst time to try and find farm work seeing as the season was almost over. I gave a long sigh. "Be glad that you don't have to deal with this kind of shit." Talking to constellations wouldn't help me. Finding another job and getting away from Kyle was the only thing that would help me.

DAY 4,399

I sat back in an old rocking chair on the porch of an old farmhouse, looking out on the endless stars once more. I didn't lie out in the fields the way I did when I was younger. This was a good vantage point to see all there was to see. I had a room in this house. It served as the barracks for the policemen in the small town of Irrigon, Oregon. It'd been four years since I'd walked away from Kyle and his parent's farm. In that time things had become more lawless. It was like things were reverting to the old west and the time of bandits was returning. I never intended to pick up a gun and fight, but the people of this small town asked for help and I needed a job. So, here I am looking out on the stars from a pretty good place.

My feet were up on the railing in front of me as I leaned back in the chair, looking out into the darkness. It was more difficult to see the stars here. There were a lot of oil lamps around to light the streets. It was a little disappointing. I'd never really needed to deal with light pollution when I was on the farm. My mind wandered to Kyle. Sometimes I wondered about him and what he was doing. He'd been my first love. Now that I looked back on it, we were too young when we'd loved and when I'd asked him to be with me forever. I realized now that it was foolish of me to have suggested that.

The front door opened and an elderly man with long, grey curls and a twirled mustache walked out onto the porch. He closed the door and the light was shut in again. The only light left was the one small lamp hanging over the front door. "I knew you'd be out here," he said as he walked over and sat on the bench next to my chair. "You're always out here staring at those stars."

"I like the stars, Paul. They remind me that there's one thing in this universe that'll be constant."

He kicked his feet up as well, "you're thinking about something, aren't you? You only stay out this late when you're thinking about something."

"Just the past," I said, "that's something that's always there too."

"That's very true. Tell me, do you remember anything about the world before the lights went out?"

"I was eight years old. I remember when the lights went out. In the dead of night. It's what caused the accident."

"The accident?"

I didn't talk about the past. No one in Irrigon knew anything about my past. There wasn't any reason to tell them. This was a small town and I was a stranger. There were only two hundred people still living around here and I wanted them to know as little about me as possible. "It's nothing. Just a car accident when I was a kid. Everyone had cars then. That was when anyone could get gas for their vehicles."

"Those were the days," Paul gave a long sigh.

"Were they easier?"

"In some ways. Electricity made things more convenient, but it gave people more distractions. Now things are less convenient, but at least we're less distracted. Things are more like they should be. Or at least that's the way I see it."

"How can this be the way things are supposed to be?"

"Life is simpler. There are no computers, or televisions or cell phones. For those of us who remember those things, this is bliss. The world is natural, the way it should be."

"You sound ridiculous," I said, "Life would be so much easier if we could do and use all those things again."

"Would it? Would they make anything better? Somehow I don't think so."

I gazed out at the stars again, "I figure I couldn't see these stars if all the lights came back on."

"That's true. They would all be lost to light pollution."

"That's a little depressing."

Paul got up from the bench and walked back toward the door. "It's late. Tomorrow we must ride out to the Walker farm and see if they need any assistance. We haven't heard from them in a couple of days. You should get some sleep, Jace."

"Thanks, Paul. I'll get up in a minute."

He opened the door and went back into the house. I continued to watch the stars as they crawled across the sky.

DAY 4,400

I wasn't the best rider, but I got from one place to another. Most people rode horses these days. Gas was hard to come by and was mostly kept in the cities. Out here in the country, we rode. The rumor was only the state police had motor vehicles. It was a beautiful last spring morning. A flock of snow geese flew overhead, making their way toward the Columbia River. It was still cold enough for there to be a bit of morning dew on the long, unkept grass along the road. The small beads of water glistened like jewels in the sunlight.

"You're quiet this morning," Paul said, "Did you eat anything this morning?"

I smiled over at him, "I've still got a lot on my mind. As for food, I forgot to eat again."

"You forgot to eat? How does someone forget to eat? I swear you don't need electricity to be distracted."

He was right about that. Last night I'd dreamed about Kyle. I couldn't help but remember those nights we'd spent together, locked together in passion under the stars. Those were beautiful times. It's why my mind kept returning to that place. "You're right. I should try to be more present."

"More present?" I looked over at Paul who looked confused as fuck. "You think you need to be more present? You sound ridiculous."

I nodded, knowing he was right. No one actually said things like that. Not out loud, anyway. I yawned loudly.

"Don't you fall asleep, kid. We have a few more miles yet to ride. Then we need to assess the situation."

"Do you think they're dead?"

"Bandits are hitting a lot of farms. They don't kill the farmers anymore because they need the farmers to keep farming. They just rob them blind and then head off into the ether."

"So, they could still be alive?"

"They could be. Sometimes that's not always the best either."

I didn't want to think about it. I'd seen what could happen and I didn't want to imagine the worse. "I just hope they're alive."

We continued down the road for another mile or so, then left it and took to the fields. Paul was hoping we could approach the farm without being seen. There was smoke in the air as we approached the edge of the tree line. That's when we saw the smoke rising from the farmhouse. "They've been hit alright," Paul said. "There's probably no one left."

"We have to go check. We can't just assume that they're lost."

Paul just sat there on his horse for a moment, surveying the land. "Whoever did this, they seem to be gone."

"Then we should go check it out."

"Seems clear enough. Let's go."

We rode up to the still smoldering farmhouse, keeping our eyes out for anything suspicious. I dismounted my horse and handed the reigns to Paul. I walked over to the door. I opened it carefully, hoping that the flames had died down. The door swung open and I stepped inside. My foot fell through the floor as I stepped on a burned floorboard. "Dammit!" Paul was there in a second, helping to pull me out of the hole. There was a jagged, wooden splinter sticking out of my knee. Paul lowered me to the floor.

"That doesn't look so good," Paul said.

I looked over my shoulder into the living room. The burned bodies of the farmer and his wife laid on the charred floor. "Neither does that. They're dead."

"I figured they probably were. There's nothing we can do about it. We need to bury them."

"I don't know if I'm in any condition to be digging."

"You're right," Paul reached down to try and help me to my feet. "We should go now. Bring back a team to assist. We were just supposed to be doing recon anyway."

I hissed as I was pulled to my feet. The pain was pretty bad. I reached down and examined my knee, "Goddamn, this thing is probably gonna get infected. Should I pull it out?"

Paul didn't answer. Instead, he slowly raised his arms in the air, a look of distress on his face. "You okay?" I asked.

"There's a gun in my back."

"What the…?"

There was then a gun in my face as masked men flooded into the room. "Put your hands up," one of them told me. I did as I was told. There was no use getting myself killed just yet. I was quickly disarmed, and my hands were bound behind me. The ruffians then threw me to the floor. Paul was thrown down next to me. We watched as the men walked through the house. A tall man with long dark hair came and stood guard over us. He didn't speak to us, but he kept looking at me with his deep green eyes. Half of his face was covered by a dark mask, but those eyes. They reminded me so much of Kyle's. But he was back on the farm.

"You should let us go," I said, "we're the law around here."

"The law?" He scoffed, "you're not very good at your job if you get all banged up and caught with your backs turned when you come to investigate."

I glared up at him, "At least we're not filthy murdering thieves like you."

The masked man kicked me in the side. I couldn't help the groan that escaped me. "Don't say anything else," Paul said, "he'll kill you."

"Listen to your old friend, boy."

I did as he said and waited quietly for the ruffians to go through the house, taking everything that was left. Our guard continued to watch me. I tried my best to ignore it. Finally, one of his men came to him, "We've been through everything. There wasn't much left."

"That's a pain in the ass. Did you find anything of use?"

"No money, no food, no fuel. Almost nothing."

"I was expecting better."

"We all did, boss. We should have gotten here first. They murdered the farmer. We never would have done that."

"Not in front of the prisoners," the boss said.

"I think we're ready to head out, boss. Anything you else?"

Then his big green eyes were on me again. "Him," he said. "Bring the young one, leave the other one."

"No!" I cried as the bandit leaned over me and lifted me over his shoulder. I could hear Paul crying out my name as I was carried away. I was taken outside and flung over the back of my own horse. Soon, the bandits were on the move and I was their captive.

***

Every inch of me hurt. They'd set me upright on my horse finally but riding bound was no picnic. I also had a gag in my mouth now. He was riding next to me. The one they called the boss. He kept looking at me, his large green eyes watching me carefully. He wanted something I didn't know what. I just hoped it wouldn't be too painful.

We finally rode into a camp down by the river. The bandits seemed to have taken over an old marina that wasn't in use anymore. There were tents set up right along the river and men, women and children bustled around the tent city. It was more like a small village than a bandit camp. The camp was lit with small oil lamps. The tents themselves were also filled with light. The horses stopped in front of the largest tent and the boss jumped off his horse. He then came over to me and lifted me off the back of my horse, keeping me slung uncomfortably over his shoulder. "Please take care of the horses," he said to his men. "I've gotta go put this down."

He carried me into his tent and sat me down in a small, wooden chair and pulled the gag out of my mouth. I couldn't help but lose my anger at him. "What do you want from me, you asshole?!"

He laughed. I wasn't expecting that reaction. "I just wanted a chance to talk to you, Jace."

"How do you know my name?" He pulled the mask off his face and I couldn't believe what I saw. "Kyle?"

"That's right, I was always hoping that I'd see you again, Jace."

"You're a bandit, Kyle? How the hell did this happen? Are your parents here?"

His eyes changed then from joy to sadness, "they were killed by bandits."

"What?" I felt sad for him then. I knew his parents were not my own, but they'd taken care of me when I needed a job and a home. "I'm sorry to hear that. When did this happen?"

"Not long after you left. I was in town when it happened. When I came home, my parents were dead, our farm was looted, and I was kidnapped by freakin' scavengers."

"Scavengers?"

"Yup. I was kidnapped by scavengers. I'm now the leader of that very band."

"How did that happen?" I was so confused about everything that was happening. This was insanity. Everything that was happening was just insane.

"I kicked the last leader's ass."

"I don't know what to make of any of this. You've become the very thing that destroyed your family."

He sat down on the bed across from me, his green eyes staring into my own. "My parents were murdered by bandits, Jace. I've never killed anyone in my life. Don't accuse me of things I've not done. I had to become what I have because I wasn't given a choice. You don't get one either."

"What?" I asked.

"Oh yeah, you're plunder. You can't just walk away from this place. Technically you were rightfully looted and are therefore my property."

"You can't do that. I'm a lawman, not a scavenger. And I'm certainly not your property."

He scoffed at me, "you can try to run away. This camp is well guarded, you won't get far. And that leg of yours means you won't be making it far anyway."

I scowled at him, "the police will come for me."

"The police? Seeing as they were so incompetent, they let you get taken in the first place, I'm not really that worried about them."

"Screw you!"

Kyle got up from the bed and put the gag back in my mouth. "We'll talk about this more in the morning." He twisted the knob on the oil lamp and put it out. Then he laid down in the darkness and was soon asleep. I sat there in the chair for a moment, thinking about my plight and wondering how I might get out of this. It wasn't going to be easy with my knee, which was currently throbbing. I gave a long sigh. I hated it when things got complicated. I closed my eyes. Seeing Kyle also complicated things. I'd never expected to see him again and yet here he was.

Sleep. Just try to sleep.

DAY 4,401

I woke to Kyle bending over in front of me and patting my face repeatedly. He pulled the gag out of my mouth. "Are you alright?"

I gave him the eye, scowling at Kyle. "I'll live. My knee still hurts, but I'll live."

"I'll have the doctor come in and look at it."

"You have a doctor?" I asked.

He nodded, "there's a person who does the best she can with what she has."

"Am I going to regret having her poke and prod me?"

"Don't be ridiculous," he stood up and walked to the opening of the tent. He beckoned to someone out there and then turned back to me. "She'll be here in a moment." He knelt next to me and examined the wound himself. "I may have to put you on the bed. Have you ever gotten stitches before?"

"Stitches?" I tried to look down at my own knee. The fear that I might lose my leg gripped me suddenly. "Does it look infected, or gangrenous?"

"Stop worrying. It doesn't look that bad. A few stitches and you should be right as rain." He lifted me and hefted me over his shoulder. I grunted in pain as he hefted me over to the bed and dumped me onto it.

"Goddammit! Will you please be gentle!"

"Have you gotten whinier?"

"Whiner?" I glared up at him, wishing that I could flip him off. "You kidnapped me and brought me here. I have a right to be a little whiny."

"Well, stop your bitching, she's coming."

The flap of the tent was thrown open and a young woman with long dark hair and fierce black eyes stormed in, crossing quickly over to the bed. To be honest, she scared me a bit as she stood over me, glowering. Her eyes went straight to the bloodied wound. She prodded it with her finger.

"Ouch!" I cried. "Watch it!"

She reached into her bag and pulled out a pair of scissors. She cut into the fabric of my trousers and cut a small section out around the wound. Upon further examination, she pulled a pair of tweezers out of her bag. She grasped the sliver of wood with the tweezers and yanked the piece of wood out of my leg. My reaction was a mere hiss of pain. It wasn't as bad as I figured it might be.

"Is he gonna need stitches?" Kyle asked.

"You love watching me sew people up, don't you?" She asked, pulling a large bandage out of her bag as well as some antiseptic. "It's painful, but it's not that bad." She put the antiseptic and the bandage on my wound, causing another hiss to escape my lips. Then, she was gone almost as quickly as she'd appeared.

"Did she have a name?" I asked as I laid on the bed, looking up at Kyle. "I think I missed it. She's really efficient, that's for sure."

"Her name is Andrea," he replied. "She's kept all of us alive."

"That's good to know. Will you please untie me? I'm not going anywhere."

He pulled a knife out of the sheath at his side and cut my bonds. "I'm not going to keep you here if you don't want to stay. I was just trying to scare you last night. There were a few things I wasn't completely honest about. I didn't beat up someone to become the leader, I wasn't taken by the scavengers. They found me and I joined them. They chose me to be their leader."

I sat up on the bed, rubbing my wrists. "Why would you lie about something like that? Are your parents even dead?"

"Yes, that part is true. I just chose to follow the scavengers when they passed through and took everything that was left behind by the damn raiders. I've just been with them ever since."

I sighed. "You chose to be a criminal? You were a farmer who knew how to work the land. There are farms that would have hired you."

"I made a choice. I don't regret it."

"But you could have been respectable."

He rolled his eyes in frustration. "Respectable?" He walked to the entrance of the tent but stopped just before stepping out. "You can leave if you like. But, if you'll stay until night, there's something you should see. That can only be seen when the sun goes down." He left the tent. I sat on the bed and thought about leaving. He'd given me permission to do so, after all. Then I realized why he'd brought me here. He wanted to see me again and talk to me. Maybe he still loved me, even after four years apart. I 'd missed him as well and wanted desperately to see him. The memory of one's first love seldom faded. I still had feelings for him and probably always would. Seeing him again hadn't been good for me. Spending more time with him wasn't going to do me any favors either.

I was curious about what he wanted to show me. I was sure it had something to do with the stars. If there was one thing that Kyle would probably never forget it was that I loved the stars. If there was one thing I would always remember about him, it was that he always liked to surprise me with something beautiful. I laid back on the bed, staring up at the canvas. For now, I would rest. I would wait to see what Kyle had in store for me. I didn't feel that he owed me anything. He certainly didn't. I'd gotten over feeling slighted by his rejection. Now I just wanted to know what Kyle was going to show me. Soon, I was dreaming of watching the stars with him. It was a good dream.

* * *

I was awakened by Kyle lighting the oil lamp sitting on the table. He was also setting out plates of food. He glanced over at me. "Are you hungry?"

I sat up on the bed and stretched, a yawn escaping me. "I slept too long."

"But I take it you're now rested."

"I'm fine."

"You just didn't want to leave."

"I'm that transparent, aren't I?"

"Well, you weren't that hurt, and your horse is in the stable. You could have just ridden away, but you chose not to." He beckoned to me, "come have something to eat."

I walked over to the little table and sat down on one of the uncomfortable wooden chairs. The food on the plate in front of me was simple. Bread, corn and a little pork chop. I was pretty good fare for nomads. Kyle sat down across from me. "We've done pretty well finding food recently. Scavenging has been good to us this year."

"Kyle, have you ever thought of giving this life up and getting a real job. Rejoining proper society?"

"Are you judging me, Jace?"

"A little bit," I said as I munched on my piece of bread. "You don't have to live like this."

"What if I want to?"

"You want to live as a thief?"

He scoffed, "We don't steal. We scavenge from people who are already dead."

"Yes, people like your parents," I reminded him. "People like my Father and me."

"Do we have to talk about this right now? I'm eating."

"We're eating. But if you want to talk about something else, go ahead."

He looked at me with his puppy-dog eyes. "I've missed you. You know that, right?"

I rolled my eyes, "this is what you want to talk about? Good lord…"

"I have. I've missed you. When you left, I thought about coming after you. I just…couldn't."

"You rejected me."

"I know. You said something about getting married and I had a freakout. People do that sometimes. I was eighteen and dumb."

"Yes, you were." I went back to my food. I didn't want to talk anymore. A little salt and pepper would have been nice, too. "has the cook ever heard of seasoning?"

"Don't start."

We ate in silence from then on. When we were done, the sun had gone down. I stepped out of the tent and looked skyward. My view was obscured by the many trees spreading out in a dark canopy overhead.

"Come with me," Kyle said as he brushed past me. I followed him. He led me down toward the river which was nothing like it was when the dams were still working. "We're just downriver of what was McNary Dam. It's not a dam so much anymore as it's just something the water passes through on its way downriver."

"I've seen it," I said, "I live in Irrigon. I've made the ride before."

"Good for you," he said as he continued to lead me along. As time went on, I began to worry about where he was leading me off to. We'd slogged through wet brush and over slick rocks and through tall grasses. Where on earth were we going?

Finally, we stepped out of the tall grass on the shore of a small lake. All the stars in the sky were reflected upon the water. The stillness of the water and the cloudless sky had brought all the stars in heavens to the earth. I walked over to the edge of the water and touched it. It was almost as if I could touch the stars themselves. "It's so beautiful."

"I knew you would like this place. It's perfect for you. It's why I chose to camp here."

I continued to gaze upon the water. Mesmerized by the endless star-scape. "I never want to leave this place."

Kyle laughed, "I thought you had to go back to your respectable life."

I sat at the water's edge. He was right. I had a life I'd told him I needed to get back to. Staying here and staring at the stars didn't factor into that life. "Why is it that every time I see you, you make things complicated?"

"I make them complicated?" Kyle sat down by the water's edge. "I guess I was the one who rejected you. I can't change the past. All I have are regrets about that."

I couldn't help but sit down by his side. Seeing him again had brought back feelings that did nothing but confuse me. I shouldn't want to be with him, but suddenly, that's the only thing I wanted. I glanced over at him in the darkness. "Remember when we used to sit together like this and just talk."

"Sure. I liked having those times with you. Just sitting back watching the stars. Life was good. I didn't know how good they were."

I put my arm around him. I shouldn't be doing this. It was dangerous territory for someone who couldn't get emotionally involved. Part of me wanted to be emotionally involved. Goddamn Kyle and his beautiful sexiness. "God it's beautiful out here."

"You're trying not to think about us."

It wasn't a question. It was as if he knew what I was thinking. "I hate it when you know my mind."

"You're predictable."

I took my arm back. "Hey! Am not…"

"Just relax, will you. You're so goddamn sensitive."

I scowled at him, offering him my arm again. "You know I still love you, right?"

"Yeah, I figured. That's why I kidnapped you. I certainly didn't have to and there are some here who wish I hadn't."

"You know the police are coming for you…eventually. For kidnapping me."

"I look forward to it."

"They'll probably think you're raiders and try to wipe you out."

He chuckled, "they can try."

"You don't think much of our skills, do you?"

"Skills?" He laughed again.

"Hey, screw you!"

"Now you're talking."

"You move at light speed, don't you?"

Another chuckle, "something has to."

I leaned in and kissed him. He responded by returning the kiss and pushing me down onto the sand. What followed was a night of passion under the endless star-scape.

DAY 4,402

I woke with his arms still wrapped around me. I snuggled into him, not wanting to open my eyes, even under the light of the morning sun. I couldn't help but wonder what time it was.

I opened my eyes. We were lying on the hard, packed sand that was now rough as I began to move. I cursed under my breath. The damn sand was going to be everywhere now. I just hoped I could get it all out. I wriggled out of Kyle's grasp and got to my feet. My clothes were scattered on the beach nearby. I dressed quickly, trying to get all the sand out of them.

I heard Kyle yawn and looked over my shoulder at him. He was still naked on the sand. "It's freezing," I said. "You should get some clothes on. We're lucky we didn't catch a cold last night."

"That's not how you catch colds," he said as he rose and began to dress.

"I enjoyed last night," I told him.

A smile crossed his face as he pulled his boots on. "I enjoyed it too."

"We should do it again."

He jumped up and joined me. "Does that mean you're going to stay?"

I paused. I didn't know how to reply to that. "I'm not sure."

"Do you believe in second chances?"

I took him into my arms. "I do. I'm just…so baffled by all this. Just, you being here and still loving me and everything."

"We should get back."

I pulled away from him. Taking his hand, we walked together back toward the camp. We were about halfway there when we heard the gunshots. "What the fuck?"

"I think they've come for me. We can't go back there."

"Those are my people! I can't abandon them."

He pulled away from me and ran toward the sound of shooting. I followed him, hoping that I could stop him before he got there. They'd kill him, of that I was sure. He was almost to the camp when several police gunmen burst through the trees on their horses. Their guns were immediately pointed at Kyle. I threw myself between him and the gunmen.

Kyle reached into the waistband of his trousers where I know he had a gun. As soon as he pulled it out, I knocked it from his hand. I punched him in the face. He fell to the ground, nearly unconscious and I turned to my fellow policemen. "We can take him. We don't have to kill him."

The policemen lowered their guns. One of them made their way forward. He was a tall man with steely blue eyes and a grim look on his face. He didn't seem to be the most interested in sparing anyone if he didn't have to. He looked like a true Western Sherriff with his cowboy hat and boots. The others were almost as stereotypical. "Jace, we're glad we found you. Why would you bother saving him?"

"Because we don't have to kill him."

"He's just going to be executed."

"Throw me some cuffs, will you?"

The policeman threw me a pair of cuffs. "What about the others at the camp?" I asked.

"Most of them fled into the woods. That's why we rode into the trees."

"Okay. I think we can go. They won't be troubling us anymore."

The Policeman rode forward and pulled Kyle onto his horse.

"My horse is in the camp," I said. "I'll go get it and we'll be off."

I went back to the camp and got my horse out of the stable. There were bodies strewn about the camp, all dead. I didn't know any of them, but their deaths were no less sad. I hoped beyond hope that I could convince them not to kill Kyle. I loved him and couldn't bear it if they killed him. I'd only just found him again. I couldn't let them take him from me.

As I caught up to the other policemen, I looked up to the front of the line and wondered if Kyle was alright. Had I saved him only to see him be killed? I cursed under my breath. I may have just made the biggest mistake of my life.

***

When we got back into town, I rode to the station with the other policemen. Kyle was taken into the station and was put into a cell in the back. I could see him through the small window in the door separating the front of the station from the room in the back where the cells were. When he saw me, he fixed me with a penetrating glare. He hated me, which was an understandable reaction. Paul was sitting behind the sheriff's desk. He looked well enough for having been tied up and left for dead just a day earlier. I made my way over to him. "Paul, I'm glad to see you're alright."

"I'm glad to see you too, kid. I was sure they woulda killed you by now. How's your leg?"

I'd completely forgotten about it. I glanced down at my leg, seeing the bandage through the hole in my trousers. "They treated it. Doesn't hurt at all."

"You're lucky it didn't get infected."

"Yeah, I got lucky. Is there going to be a trial for the prisoner?"

Paul looked confused, "why would we give him a trial. It's pretty straight forward. He's a raider."

"No, he's not," I replied, "he's a scavenger. Technically, that's not the same thing. He may be a thief, but he didn't kill anyone."

"He kidnapped you, kid. That's a crime. Why would you want to save him?"

"Well, he may be a kidnapper, but he didn't hurt me. Doesn't he deserve due process of the law?"

Paul rolled his eyes, "He tied me up, he kidnapped you. If no one had come along to help me, I might have died in that farmhouse. Luckily, another group of policemen came after us when we didn't come back. If I'd died..."

"It's still the law that he gets a trial and his chance to tell his side."

Paul gave me the eye. He was angry with me, and I guess I could understand that. "I'll talk to the Captain when he gets back. We'll see what he has to say about this."

"Alright, thank you, Paul," I said, "I'm going to go talk to the prisoner."

"Fine, kid," Paul sounded annoyed as he kicked his cowboy boots up on the desk. "Knock yourself out."

I nodded. I made my way to the back room. Kyle was in the first cell and gave me a vicious glare when I walked in. "Don't give me that look," I said. "I couldn't let them kill you. I just couldn't."

"You're a fucking idiot. They're going to kill me and there's no way out of it."

"I asked about you getting a trial."

"A trial?" Kyle threw his arms up in frustration. "People like me don't get trials. We get executed. You should have just let them kill me there in the forest. At least then I could have died fighting."

"Died fighting?" Was that truly what he wanted? Was that what he still wanted? It was probably better than being hanged. I'd screwed him out of the death that he wanted. "I'm sorry. I guess it was my time to be selfish and assholic."

"Yeah, but your assholery is going to get me killed." He went over and sat on the small cot against the back wall of the cell which was the back wall of the station as well. He looked forlornly at the bars that surrounded him on two sides. "I can't get out of this place. Not on my own. You could help me, but you're not going to because you're more of a lawman than you are a lover. It's too bad. I thought for a moment that we could start over and be together forever."

"I'm so sorry."

"Keep your fucking sorry. It can't help me nor change what's happened."

"I love you, Kyle."

"I love you too. Sadly, love can't make this better."

I walked out of that place because I couldn't help the tears that threatened to come to my eyes. I couldn't let him see me cry. It was not about looking weak. It was about him needing to stay strong. Now I was faced with a choice. Even if he did get a trial, what he'd done was indefensible and they hanged people for less in these difficult days. I could get him out of that place, but not without breaking the law myself. Neither of these options was good. It didn't matter though. They were the only options and I was the one who had to make the decision.

* * *

I sat that night in the chair I'd sat in less than a week ago before heading out and finding Kyle again. The night was cold and clear, and the stars were out in all their glory. I stared up at them, but they brought me no comfort tonight. I'd screwed up, or at least it seemed like it. I hated myself. Maybe I should. There was nothing I could save the one I loved; the last person on earth that loved me back.

Someone came and sat on the bench next to me. I'd figured it was Paul, but it wasn't. It was the Captain, a grim-looking old man whose craggy wrinkles I could make out even in the dark. He gave a long sigh as he sat down. Whatever he had on his mind was annoying him. "I hear you want to give the murdering thief we captured a trial. His crimes are clear; why would you ask for a trial in such an open and closed case?"

"He's not a murderer. He's just a scavenger."

"Doesn't matter. Kid's still a thief and we can't have that either. Thieves have to pay for their crimes as well."

"He didn't want to die this way. I did this to him."

"Why do you even care, boy? He's common scum."

"How do you know that?"

"Because these assholes are all the same. Killers, thieves, monsters. If we were to give this kid a trial, we'd have to take him to the county seat in Heppner which would be a literal pain in the ass. It's too much trouble for scum like him."

"Too much trouble?"

"This is a hard world, kid."

I kicked the railing in anger, my foot nearly breaking the wooden beam. "You think I don't know that? That I don't know how screwed up and hard things are? My mother was in a car accident the night the lights went out. She was still alive, but only just. She was kept alive in the hospital for a while in the hospital with machines. When the generators died because there was no more gas, she died. My Father who hoped she might wake up had prolonged her suffering for nothing. Then when I was sixteen, he was murdered right in front of me, in broad daylight, on the city street. The law in that city blamed gangs, but they never looked for the murderers. They felt they didn't have to. That's when I fled the city for the country. Then years of farm labor until I finally made my way here after being rejected by my lover. I was ready to try and love him again, and now you're threatening to take him away again?"

I heard him chuckle in his low gravelly voice. "So, you know this asshole?"

I'd messed up again, revealing that I knew Kyle. "I do..."

"Let me guess. That's why you don't want us to kill him. Because you're still hoping to ride off into the sunset with him?"

"Is that really so terrible?"

"Nah, not really. I think we all dream of living happily ever after with the one we love. The problem with this is, he's a fucking criminal."

I glanced over at him, smiling. "No one is perfect, sir. I'm certainly not."

"That may be true, but we don't have the time or resources to escort a prisoner to Heppner right now. We're responsible for bringing this young man to justice."

"I don't care about justice."

"Isn't that a little selfish of you?"

I shrugged, "probably. What do you want from me?"

He sighed, "I'm sorry, kid. The criminal's being executed tomorrow."

"What if I pay for his freedom?"

"Pay for his freedom? What do you think this is? You wouldn't have that kind of money anyway."

I nodded, though I knew he couldn't see it. It didn't matter. "I'll be gone in the morning."

"Don't do anything foolish, kid."

"I wouldn't dream of it," I said.

The Captain got up off the bench, looking back over his shoulder, "I think it's a good time to try and sleep. Sweet dreams, kid."

"Sweet dreams to you as well, sir," I said.

He went inside and put out the oil lamps. I was plunged into complete darkness. If I was going to do something, now was the time. There wouldn't be another opportunity. I just needed one more moment to try and figure out what that something was. I looked out on the stars again. Tonight, they felt like they were far more distant, and I was truly alone in the wide universe.

***

I was alone, alright. And if anyone was going to have to find a way out of this for Kyle, it was me. I went to the stables, and in the near-complete darkness, I saddled two horses. I knew my way around horses enough to know what to do. They were just a bit miffed that I was bothering their sleep. Once they were saddled and ready, I led them out to the front of the jail. There would only be one man on guard in there. It'd be Paul and I hoped beyond hope that I wouldn't have to shoot him as I turned the brass knob that would open that fateful door. I didn't like what I was about to do, but there was little choice if I was going to save Kyle.

I threw open the door, drawing my gun and stepping into the front room of the station. And there was Paul, still sitting behind the desk, shaking his head groggily as I made my entrance. He cocked his head at me, and I cocked mine in reply. "Were you asleep at your station?"

"Never mind that," he said, noticing the gun in my hand. "Are you trying to break that criminal out of jail?"

"I asked first."

He sighed, giving me the stink eye. "You know this is a bad idea, right? That it's going to make you a criminal, too?"

I nodded. I knew what I was doing and that it was the worst thing I could do. It wasn't going to stop me, though. "I'm sorry. I just ran out of time and options. Put your gun on the table and get the keys."

"Well, kid, you've got the drop on me. I don't think you'd want to shoot me, but I also don't think that means you won't."

"You're right. God, I don't wanna shoot you, Paul. That's why it would be a good idea to let us both just walk out of here."

"Wouldn't that make me an accomplice?"

"Not if you say I made you. Which is pretty much what I'm doing."

The older man nodded. I think in the end he knew why I was doing this and that this could end up in him not living to tell the tale. Paul set his gun down on the desk and he grabbed the keys. "I figure I've got no choice, then."

"I figure you're right. Now go to the back and get him. I'll follow and watch from the door."

"I think you realize by now that I'm not going to try and stop you."

I smiled, "yeah, I know. I appreciate it."

He walked over to the door leading back to the cells and opened it with the keys. I then watched from the doorway as he went to the cell door and released Kyle. Kyle was resting on the cot in his cell. When he heard the keys clinking, he rolled over and sat up, a look of confusion on his face. When he looked over and saw me standing there with a gun in hand, he rose and walked to the door of the cell, waiting anxiously for it to open. Once he was out, I said to Paul, "give him the keys and get inside."

The older man rolled his eyes at me. "Really?"

"We need a head start."

Paul gave Kyle the keys and stepped into the cell. He was soon locked inside.

Kyle came to my side, then. He put his hand on my arm. "Are you sure you want to do this? You'd be throwing away everything."

"Yes, I'm okay with that."

"If you're sure."

"Will you two assholes just get out of here?" Paul called from the cell as he fixed us with his most annoyed old man glare.

We did, making our way out of the station and to the horses. After that, we disappeared into the darkness, guided only by the endless stars.

DAY 4,404

After riding all that night and into the day, we found ourselves at the base of the Blue Mountains in Eastern Oregon. By the time the sun was getting ready to end once again, we were camping in the town of Meachum, which was at the top of Cabbage hill. We'd passed out of the endless fields and desert and had finally found the thick forest in the mountains. The tall pines swayed gently in the cool mountain breeze as we sat beside a cozy fire. Meachum wasn't so much a town as it was one abandoned store that's gone out of business long ago. No one really stopped here and when they did, they camped like Kyle and I were doing.

Right now, he was lounging next to the fire across from me, picking his teeth with his fingernail. "That rabbit was tough."

"There was not much fat on it," I replied, my back up against a damp log. It wasn't damp enough to soak through my clothes, nor dry enough that it didn't smell like moss and the summer rain. "Tough meat is always a pain in the ass."

"Yeah, it is."

One of the horses snorted in the darkness, causing Kyle to jump like a scared bunny. He was paranoid about every noise he heard. "You don't think they'll come for us?"

I huffed, "of course, they're going to come for us. But I doubt they'll be able to catch up by the time we reach the border. They can't pursue us past the state border."

"But they can report us to the authorities in that state."

"And by the time they do, we'll be in yet another state."

He laughed at me, "You're always so optimistic." His smile then faded. "You don't regret what happened, do you?"

I hadn't taken any time to really think about it. There just hadn't been the time to think about it. "I…don't regret anything. I can't. Even if I did, it wouldn't change anything. I'd still be here with you and I'm fine with that. In fact, I'm happy that I found you again and I'm happier that we get to spend the rest of our lives together." I rose from my spot and walked around the fire. Sitting down next to him, I curled into him. He put his arm securely around me and for the first time in days I felt safe. "I love you. I've always loved you. The only thing I've ever regretted is walking away from your farm the day we parted."

"I didn't even realize what I'd lost."

"Of course, you didn't," I chuckled, "sometimes you're not very smart."

"Hey! What do you mean not very smart?"

"Pft, stop it. Just lay back and watch the stars with me," I replied. The stars were slightly drowned out by even the light of our little campfire. Still, I could see them clearly. They were always there and always would be. Now I would watch them for the rest of my life with my Kyle by my side.

Other titles by the authors that you may enjoy:

Soul of a Vampire
By Silencio Marquez

Kris Kellman is a vampire living in Calgary, Canada who works as a detective at the Magical Laws Division. It's his job to solve crimes committed by magical people like himself. When his former lover, Zeke Yonah, shows up on his doorstep covered in blood and asking for help, Kris is conflicted. Is he a vampire first, or is he a cop?

As he begins to investigate the murder that Zeke doesn't remember committing, things get really complicated when Kris realizes that Zeke is being set up for murder.

Charles Anderson is in charge of the vampire community, and he has a plan to enslave all mankind. The only thing standing in his way are people like Zeke and Kris, a vampire whose loyalty can't be bought. Kris's ridiculous dragon-shifter boyfriend isn't making things easier either.

Kris realizes that if he can't stop Charles, it will mean war between humans and vampires. He knows that it's not just humans that will suffer, but vampires like him who won't just sit by and let Charles get away with genocide. Will Kris do what's right and bring Charles to justice before it's too late?

Diary of a Vigilante
By Shaun Curtis

'Before you embark on a journey of revenge, dig two graves'.

It's a blurred line between hero and villain, between vigilante and criminal, between decent citizen and maniac - and this is where Jack finds himself. Jack is a man haunted by the failures of a justice system he feels is broken and the seemingly arbitrary punishments measured out to those who have offended the state.

When his friend's family find themselves threatened by a sexual predator and let down by the police, Jack snaps, and a journey of vigilantism, anger and revenge pursues. Told from his point of view, the **Diary of a Vigilante**, Jack descends further into the pits of the underworld, and the man who set out to clean the streets, finds that *he* becomes the top target of law enforcement.

What price will Jack pay for his vengeance, and in a world of eye-for-an-eye justice, what sort of man will he be at the end? Will he become the very same monster he sought to destroy?

Arc City Stories
By various authors

Welcome to Arc City.

A city that exists in a world beyond governments, where war and climate change have destroyed the old order. Corporations are now the authorities of the surviving city states. The elite live in luxury above the clouds in their towers, everyone else lives further down, based on their corporate and economic worth.

Arc City Stories is an exciting, action-packed collection of nine cyberpunk tales, written by eight authors, of various citizens each trying to survive, in their own way, this brave new world.

Love You to Death
By Max McCamish

Alex Keen has never felt anything. No sadness, no happiness, no anger, and certainly no love; that's the way Alex prefers it. One day, a chance encounter changes everything, and suddenly emotionless, empty Alex is developing painful, longing feelings for someone- and that just won't do. So, like everyone else who's gotten in Alex's way before, there seems to be just one thing to do to the man Alex suddenly loves: kill him.

Of course, killing the one and only person you've ever loved isn't that simple, and a past riddled with murder is going to get noticed. One of Alex's past victims has family left behind who want revenge, and even with unexpected help, Alex's options for dealing with the justice closing in on them are slim- especially when they're in the middle of committing another murder.

But Alex has to kill him. How else are they meant to escape the pain of love?

A Storm of Magic
By Ashley Laino

Being brought back from the dead is an impressive trick, even for magician Darien Burron. Now he must try and use his sleight of hand to swindle modern-day witch, Mirah, to sign her power away, or end up a tormented demon in the afterlife.

Meanwhile, sixteen-year-old Mirah is starting to lose control of her powers. After an incident at her aunt's Witchery store, Mirah is sent to a secret coven to learn to control her abilities.

While away, Mirah meets up with a soft-spoken clairvoyant, a brazen storm witch, and the creator of dark magic itself. The young woman must learn to trust in herself before she loses herself entirely to the darkness that hunts her.

Consumed
By Justin Alcala

Sergeant Nathaniel Brannick is trapped in Victorian London during a period of disease, crime, and insatiable vices. One night, Brannick returns from work to find an eerie messenger in his flat who warns him of dark things to come.

When his next case involves a victim who suffered from consumption, he uncovers clues that lead him to believe the messenger's warning. Despite his incredulity, he can't help but wonder if the practical man he once was has been altered by an investigation encompassed in the paranormal. That is, until he meets the witch hunters, and everything takes a turn for the worse.

Dusty Plains & Wartime Planes
By John Wait Jr. & John S. Wait

The men and women who fought in World War II are often referred to as "The Greatest Generation," and for good reason. Before ever stepping onto the battlefield, most had survivedThe Great Depression, and if they happened to live in the Midwest, The Dust Bowl. Such was the case with my father. Dad grew up in poverty in rural Kansas with no electricity or plumbing, not even an outhouse. While in college he became a pilot, and then joined the Army Air Force shortly before WWII. For someone who never fired a gun or received enemy gunfire, he had one of the most amazing service records. He managed two of the most famous airfields in the world – Heathrow and Le Bourget -- then became one of the first Americans to visit Hitler's bunker only a couple of days after his suicide.

From Dusty Plains to Wartime Planes is educational, moving and highly entertaining. This first person account includes some of the most famous periods and places in our nation's history, including the Dust Bowl, The Great Depression, World War II, Heathrow, Normandy, Le

Bourget, and Hitler's Bunker. The storyline is supplemented with historical notes and fascinating photos.

BLKDOG

www.blkdogpublishing.com